The Legend of Tabby Hollow

by

Kathi Daley

Chapter 1

Monday, October 19

The hollow is a mystical place located in the center of Madrona Island. Given the rocky cliffs that encircle the area, it is protected from the storms that ravage the shoreline. The hollow is uninhabited except for the cats who reside in the dark spaces within the rocks. While most of the island's residents stop short of referring to the hollow as haunted, it is widely accepted that not everything that happens there can be explained.

I enjoy the pilgrimage I make to the area on a monthly basis. After Aunt Maggie founded Harthaven Cat Sanctuary, I took on the role of guardian to the island's cats. When visitors first come to our island they're surprised to see such a large feral cat population. Most assume the immigrants who settled the island four generations ago brought the cats, but the truth of the matter is that the cats of Madrona Island were here before the founding families arrived.

No one knows for certain how the cats came to be on the island, but local legend tells of a man named Ivan Valtranova. Ivan was a merchant from Russia who supposedly found the island when he was blown off course during a storm. He took refuge in the hollow with the twelve cats with whom he traveled. If folklore is to be believed, he fell in love with the beauty and isolation of the island and decided to stay after the storm had passed. Most assume the cats Ivan brought with him served as the base from which the current cat population was bred.

According to the story, Ivan lived alone on the island for a number of years, until the founding families arrived and built the fishing village of Harthaven. It is said that one of the settlers killed the Russian over a land dispute. Although the account of his demise has most likely been sensationalized, it seems that after a hard-fought battle to retain his isolation, he was beheaded and his headless body was left in the hollow. The legend tells us that the head was never found and is in fact buried within the hollow. There are those who believe Ivan's spirit is trapped in the hollow and that he still wanders the area, looking for his head and exacting his revenge on those who would disturb his solitude.

Personally, I hope the legend isn't true. I don't want to believe that one or more of the founding fathers killed the man in cold blood in order to steal the land he claimed. And, although I come to the hollow on a regular basis, I've never been bothered by Ivan or any other spirit. But most legends are based at least in part on reality, and anyone who has been around for any length of time will tell you that there have been a number of strange and unexplained deaths in the area over the years.

Whatever their origin, the cats of Madrona Island are considered to be part of its charm. They were allowed to wander freely until Mayor Bradley lost several of his prize koi to the cats, motivating him to pass a law making it legal to remove the feral animals from ones' property by any means necessary. When Aunt Maggie realized the cats were in danger of being trapped and killed, she founded the sanctuary as a refuge for the beautiful and graceful animals.

Today, I chose to abandon any thoughts of death or vengeance from beyond the grave and concentrate on the beauty surrounding me. One of the things I like best about the hollow is the whispers in the air. Most believe the sound is created as the wind echoes through the canyon, but I believe the whispers are the cats, heralding my arrival.

I took my time as I walked along the narrow footpath, looking for signs of felines in distress. More often than not I leave the cats to their own devices, but occasionally I come across a tabby who is sick or injured. When this occurs I trap it and take it back to the sanctuary, where it can receive medical attention. Occasionally, I'll come across a cat who seems ripe for domestication, but most of the time I return the healed cats to the place in which I found them.

Today, I've come to the hollow for a very specific purpose. Today, I've been sent to find a messenger. Tansy hadn't given me a lot of information about him, other than that he would meet me in the hollow and lead me to that which was mine to find.

Tansy and her best friend, Bella, are rumored to be witches. Neither Tansy nor Bella will confirm or deny their witchy status, but both women know things that can't be empirically explained. Bella and Tansy live in the touristy village of Pelican Bay, which is located on the southern end of the island. The women own and operate Herbalities, a specialty shop dealing in herbs and fortune telling. While both Bella and Tansy seem to be more in tune with the natural rhythms of the universe than most, it's Tansy who demonstrates a level of intuition that's downright disturbing.

While venturing into the hollow to meet a feline messenger may seem like an odd thing to do, Tansy and her cats had never misled me in the past. I don't really understand why I've been tasked with the responsibility, but I know deep in my soul that working with the cats is my calling and destiny.

"Ichabod?" I asked the large black cat with glowing green eyes and pointy ears who had wandered onto the path in front of me.

The cat didn't answer, but somehow I knew I'd found my messenger.

"Tansy said to follow you, so here I am," I said aloud. "Lead the way."

The cat looked me up and down before he turned and started up the rocky trail that didn't appear to lead anywhere. The trail was steep and covered in shale, creating a difficult and dangerous passage. I run with my dog Max almost every day, so I'm well equipped for a laborious hike, but the sun had already begun its descent and I was concerned that the darkness would arrive before I was able to make my way back down the trail and out of the hollow. Still, over time I've learned to trust the felines Tansy sends my way, so I dutifully followed in spite of the risk.

The trail narrowed as it wound steeply up the mountain. My legs burned as I struggled to keep my footing on the unstable ground. The trip back down the path wasn't going to be fun at all.

Once I arrived at the summit, I paused to catch my breath and admire the view. The setting sun glistened off the still water of the ocean as seabirds glided above the surface, looking for their evening meal. It was too bad I hadn't thought to bring a flashlight. I imagined that sitting atop the rocky bluff as the sun set with only the cats for company would be a magical experience.

Apparently, Ichabod wasn't the patient sort because after only a minute's rest, he began meowing at me to continue the journey. I figured we must be coming to the end of the journey because it wouldn't be long before we would run out of trail. I turned away from the spectacular view and continued to follow the cat. He led me inland just a bit and then back toward the sea.

I'm not entirely certain why no one has ever developed this part of the island. I imagine it could be due to the rough terrain, although, while the current trail system is perilous at best, it wouldn't be all that hard to run a road into the interior of the unpopulated space. There's a rough dirt road that runs along the perimeter of the hollow. Most use it to access the area before continuing on foot.

I supposed the legend could also play into the equation. Most islanders won't admit to believing in the power of Ivan's ghost, yet few seem willing to put the legend to the test.

Ichabod stopped and sat down at the point where the trail met the edge of the cliff. I wasn't a huge fan of heights, but I walked up beside him and looked over the threshold. Lying at the bottom of the bluff was the body of Mayor Bradley. At least I thought it was Mayor Bradley. It was hard to know for certain because the face of the victim gave evidence to the fact that scavengers live in the area. But the body was dressed in the same suit I'd seen Mayor Bradley wear on many occasions.

Chapter 2

Wednesday, October 21

"A soy latte and a cranberry nut muffin for Jan," I called out after my best friend and business partner Tara O'Brian set the order on the counter.

"Is Hank here today?" Jan asked as she paid for her order.

"He is. I'm sure he'll be happy to see you."

"I wish I could adopt him, but until I can find a rental that allows cats I'm afraid the best I can do is visit."

"It's hard when you're first getting started. Most rentals in the area don't allow pets. I'm sure Hank would love to find a forever home, but in the meantime I know he enjoys spending time with you."

"I keep thinking that if I could save enough money I could afford to rent a house. Most of my friends who are in houses are allowed pets; it's the apartment owners who seem to be picky about animals on the premises."

"Maybe a roommate?" I suggested. "A two-bedroom house wouldn't be much more expensive to rent than a one bedroom, but you'd only have half the expense."

"That's a good idea. I might ask around to see if any of my friends are interested. This is usually a good time of year to find a rental, now that the summer crowds are gone."

"I'll keep an eye out and let you know if I hear of anything," I promised.

I watched as Jan walked toward the cat lounge. Coffee Cat Books is a unique venture Tara and I own and operate. It combines a bookstore with a coffee bar and a cat lounge, where customers can choose to visit with the cats I bring from Harthaven Cat Sanctuary each day. The idea is that the visitors will fall in love with the cats while sipping a latte and sampling the newest best seller. In most cases that's exactly what happens and the cats are adopted into forever homes.

"The lady over by the new arrivals has some questions," our new employee, Destiny Paulson, informed Tara and me. "I can cover here if one of you wants to go talk to her."

"I'll go," Tara offered. "The crowd from the ferry has pretty much cleared out, so things should slow down until the next boat docks."

"Do you have class today?" I asked. Destiny was being homeschooled by Sister Mary of St. Patrick's Catholic Church so she wouldn't fall behind during her pregnancy.

"Later," Destiny answered. "Sister Mary is busy this week because she's covering for Father Kilian, who's on vacation until Sunday."

"That should work out fine. We can head over early and grab dinner at Antonio's. I just need to pop in and talk to Finn first."

Ryan Finnegan—Finn to his friends—is the resident deputy for Madrona Island.

"Did he ever figure out how Mayor Bradley ended up in the hollow?" Destiny wondered.

"No. At this point it seems equally possible that he tripped and fell, committed suicide, or was pushed. Finn didn't find any evidence that another person was involved, but he really has no way to rule that out either."

"But why the hollow?" Destiny asked. "Mayor Bradley hated the cats and he didn't seem the type to enjoy strenuous hiking. It doesn't make sense that he'd be there in the first place."

"I've been wondering the same thing," I confided.

"Did you ever find the cat?" Destiny asked.

"No. Not yet."

After I found Mayor Bradley's body I immediately looked around for a place where I could get cell reception so I could call Finn. Ichabod had slipped away while I was looking, and I couldn't find him after Finn arrived. I sensed that our time together wasn't yet over, so I'd returned to the hollow twice looking for him, so far with no luck.

"Chances are if he's meant to help you he'll come to you," Destiny pointed out. "Based on what Tara has told me, the other cats found you rather than the other way around."

"You have a point. I just wish I knew if my role in this whole thing is complete or if I'm supposed to be doing something more."

"Like what?" Destiny asked.

"I really don't know. If we knew for certain that Mayor Bradley had been pushed, I would say that my role might be to help Finn find the killer. But if he simply slipped and fell, or if he intentionally committed suicide, there's really nothing to investigate."

"It seems a little unlikely that Mayor Bradley would choose to surround himself with cats if he planned to intentionally end his life," Destiny said.

"That's true. I guess we can assume he either slipped or was pushed."

"He had to have had a really good reason to be in the hollow in the first place," Destiny reasoned. "I bet he was either looking for something or meeting someone."

"That makes sense."

"If you feel like you want to do something to help Finn you should see if you can figure out why the mayor was on the top of that cliff in the first place."

I smiled. "How'd you get to be so smart?"

"I've always been smart. I just happened to make some bad decisions along the way and now I'm single and pregnant."

Poor Destiny really had gotten herself into a complicated situation, but she seemed to be handling it okay these days, considering. When Destiny told her mother she was pregnant she'd been understandably upset, which had led to conflict between mother and daughter to the point that Destiny had decided to run away. Luckily, I'd seen her waiting for the ferry and had been able to convince her to stay.

"By the way, did you meet with the woman at the adoption agency?" I asked.

"Yes."

"And?"

Destiny shrugged. "I don't know. All I agreed to do was talk with her, which I did. I'm still not sure I want to give my baby away. It feels like such an important decision and I feel like I'm being pressured to make a commitment one way or the other before I've really had a chance to consider all my options."

"I suppose everyone feels it would be better if you made a decision before the baby is born."

"Yeah. I guess I can see that." Destiny sighed. "I know that raising a baby on my own will be hard, but I'll be seventeen next month and I'm sure Sister Mary would help me get a GED if I don't graduate. Tara said I can stay with her as long as I want, even after the baby's born. I don't know if keeping the baby is the right decision, but I want to at least think things through."

I gave Destiny's arm a squeeze. "I don't blame you. It's a big decision, one that you'll need to live with for the rest of your life. I think you should take your time."

"Thanks, Cait. You and Tara have been great. I just wish my mom would be a bit more open-minded. She's determined to have me give my baby away."

"Your mom knows what it's like to have to raise kids on your own. I'm willing to bet she just wants to protect you from having such a difficult life."

"Maybe, but I'm not sure that giving away my baby will guarantee that my life will be easy."

"True."

I turned toward the window as the midday ferry made its way into the harbor and began lining up to dock. The crowds had decreased considerably during the week now that school was back in session and the temperatures had cooled, but we did seem to be enjoying steady business the five days a week we decided to be open during the winter. I know there are those who think a coffee bar and bookstore should be open seven days a week, but Tara and I were doing well enough to cover our costs while cutting back to

Tuesday through Saturday hours during the off season. I turned away from the window and began gathering the supplies I'd need for customers looking for a midday coffee.

One of the things I love the most about the venture Tara and I run is that I get to spend my day surrounded by books. Ironically enough, I'd had little time to read since we opened the store, but the glossy covers that stared back at me from artfully decorated bookshelves feel like old friends lying in wait for a stormy day and a much-longed-for visit.

"Isn't that your sister?" Destiny asked.

I turned back to the window. "It is. I wonder what she's doing here."

"Maybe she wanted to come for a visit. It's beautiful on the island this time of year. I hear leaf season is supposed to be at its absolute peak this weekend."

I frowned. Siobhan didn't care about leaves and she rarely came for a visit. If she was here something was most likely wrong. "Cover for me. I'll be right back."

I took off my Coffee Cat Books apron, then informed Tara that Siobhan was here and I was going to take a short break. I headed out the door and jogged over to where my sister was talking to one of the other passengers who had just gotten off the ferry. Siobhan is the second oldest Hart sibling, right after my brother Aiden. She lived in Seattle and I hadn't seen her in months. I try to get her to visit more often, but she'd be the first to tell you that she doesn't have the time to make the trip due to her many professional and social commitments. Personally, I think her avoidance of the island has more to do with the fact that she doesn't get along with my mother than it does with her busy schedule.

Siobhan is three years older than me. When we were growing up she was a good sister who looked out for me. We were actually fairly close because I was the only other girl until my sister Cassie was born when I was ten. I idolized Siobhan. She was the person I aspired to be.

I'd been crushed when Siobhan quite unexpectedly decided to accept a job in Seattle despite the fact that she was engaged to marry Finn. The two of them had dated all through high school, so he was around the house a lot of the time, and I thought of him as some sort of additional big brother. I'd really been looking forward to him becoming part of the family and was devastated when I found out he never would be.

"What are you doing here?" I hugged my sister and, surprisingly, she hugged me back. Siobhan wasn't the demonstrative type; usually the most you could expect from her was a halfhearted pat on the back.

"I just decided it was time for a visit."

I was sure Siobhan wasn't telling me everything, but I didn't push.

"Are you staying at Mom's?" I wondered.

"Actually, I was hoping to stay with Maggie. I called earlier and left a message, but she hasn't called me back."

"Maggie is away on a yoga retreat. They don't allow phones there, so I doubt she even got your message. I'm sure she won't mind if you want to crash in one of her guest rooms, though." I hugged Siobhan again. "I'm so excited you're here."

"Is that your new store?" Siobhan nodded toward Coffee Cat Books.

I nodded and took Siobhan's hand. "Come on. I want to show it to you."

I picked up Siobhan's suitcase while she positioned her purse and her computer bag over her shoulder. Although Siobhan and I haven't been superclose since she moved away, I've really missed her. Tara and Destiny greeted her, and then I showed her around the store.

"So what do you think?" I asked after giving her the grand tour.

"It's nice."

"Nice?"

Siobhan sighed. "It's great. Really. I'm just tired. Do you think you could give me a ride over to Maggie's?"

"Sure." I have to admit I was disappointed Siobhan wasn't more excited about the store Tara and I had poured our heart and soul into. Not that I expected her to be over-the-top complimentary. Ever since she'd moved away it seemed as if Siobhan tended to spend most of her time thinking about Siobhan and didn't seem all that interested in anyone or anything else.

I explained what I was doing to Tara, then led Siobhan to my clunker of a car and headed toward the peninsula, where Maggie and I live. "So how long can you stay?" I asked.

"I'm not sure."

"It's nice you were able to take time off from your job. It seems like it's been forever since I've seen you."

Siobhan smiled a little half smile but didn't respond.

"I've really missed you."

Siobhan continued to look out the side window of the car, as she'd been doing since we left the bookstore.

"Are you still dating that musician?" I asked, hoping to hit on a topic she might be interested in discussing.

"No. We broke up. How long is Maggie going to be away?"

"Through the weekend. If you get bored staying alone at Maggie's you can crash at my place, or I'm sure Mom would love to see you."

"Maggie's will be fine."

I could tell there was something Siobhan wasn't telling me, but I decided not to ask about it. Over the years I'd learned to tread lightly with my big sister. Siobhan was an independent sort who didn't take kindly to anyone meddling in her business.

"Did you hear that Mayor Bradley died?" I asked, changing the topic to something a little less personal.

Siobhan turned and looked at me. "No. What happened?"

I explained about finding him at the bottom of the cliff in the hollow.

"That is so weird. Bradley hated cats. Why would he even be in the hollow?"

"That's the question everyone is asking. I have choir practice tonight, but I thought I'd stop off to talk to Finn on the way. He might have an update on the situation."

Siobhan turned back to the window, but not before I saw an odd expression cross her face. "How is Finn?"

I frowned. It was uncharacteristic of Siobhan to ask about him, and even more unlike her to care how he was doing.

"He's good."

"Is he dating anyone?"

"No one serious as far as I know."

"I'm surprised he hasn't settled down by now. He was in such a hurry to get married and have a house full of kids when we were dating."

I turned onto the peninsula road. "Yeah, well, I guess he hasn't found the right person. How about you? You said you broke up with the musician. Is there a new guy in your life?"

"No. I'm painfully single at the moment. I heard you're dating Cody West."

"Cody and I are friends who occasionally participate in datelike activities, but I'm not sure I would say we're dating," I answered.

I pulled into the drive and parked in front of Maggie's house. Our aunt had inherited the house and the land on which it sat from her father, who had inherited it from his father. Although Maggie lived alone, the house was enormous.

"The guy is a catch," Siobhan commented as she stepped out of the car. "I know you like to take things slowly, but if I were you and I found a guy who seemed just right for me, I'd be sure to move things along before someone else came along and snatched him up."

Maybe Siobhan had a point. Cody and I had been living in relationship limbo ever since he'd moved back to the island. We spent a lot of time together and got along fantastically. I know there's chemistry between us. I'm not really sure why neither of us has taken the initiative to move things along to the next level.

"Thanks, Siobhan," I said as I retrieved her bags from the backseat. "I guess part of me has been thinking the same thing; maybe I just needed to hear someone say it out loud."

Siobhan smiled. A genuine smile. "That's what big sisters are for."

Chapter 3

"This is really nice," I commented as Cody and I walked hand in hand down the beach with my dog Max and Mr. Parsons's dog Rambler running along beside us. Cody had moved into the third floor of Mr. Parsons's house when he moved back to the island, and it just happened to be down the beach from the cabin where I lived on Aunt Maggie's property.

"It is a beautiful evening," Cody agreed, "although I'm afraid the exceptional weather we've been having may not last long. I hear rain is in the forecast."

"That's too bad. I'm not quite ready for our Indian summer to end." I'd noticed there was a chill to the air that hadn't been present since the previous winter. "I hope it doesn't rain on Sunday. The kids seemed really excited about their baseball game against the parents when we were talking about it tonight. Besides, I was hoping to convince Siobhan to come so she could see everyone. It's been forever since she's been home."

"Did you tell Finn she's in town?"

"Yes. I'm afraid I made the mistake of mentioning it when I first arrived at his office and then I couldn't get him to focus on the case at all. I feel so bad for him. It's obvious he's still in love with her in spite of the way she treated him."

I couldn't help but think back to the spring Siobhan had left the island. Cody had already gone, creating a hole of sorts in my heart, but when Siobhan up and deserted both Finn and the family, I was devastated. Of course Finn was even more heartbroken than I was, and I guess in a way it brought us even closer together. No matter what happens between Finn and Siobhan, he'll always feel like family to me.

"I was surprised when I heard they split," Cody commented. "They always seemed so good together. What happened anyway?"

"I'm not sure," I said. "One minute they were engaged and Mom was busy planning the wedding of the decade, and the next thing I knew Siobhan had announced she'd been offered a job in Seattle and was moving immediately. I thought she might ask Finn to go with her, but she didn't. When I asked her about it she said her job was going to be really intense, so she needed to focus all of her attention on it."

"I guess that sort of makes sense."

"Maybe. But the thing is, while Siobhan hasn't entered into a serious relationship since she's been living in Seattle, she does date a lot. It seems like dating would be pretty distracting as well."

"Not necessarily," Cody countered. "Relationships can take an emotional toll on a person, while casual dating can help you unwind without all the messy emotions."

"So you think serious relationships can be distracting while casual dating isn't?"

"Sometimes."

Cody and I settled into a temporary silence as the cold water washed over our feet. I was bundled up in sweatpants and a sweatshirt, but I was still going to need to toss a match on the fire I'd laid earlier in the day when I got home. The drop in temperature once the sun sets makes for a chilly evening.

"So what do you think about our case?" I asked, deciding that I really didn't want to think about the casual relationships Cody must have entered into during the years we were apart.

"Do we have a case?" Cody asked.

I hesitated. Did we? I really wasn't sure.

"I don't know; maybe, maybe not. Destiny suggested today that we should focus on trying to find out why the mayor was on the cliff in the hollow in the first place. I'm not sure how we're going to be able to tell why he fell, but if we can determine why he was in the area that could give us a clue as to what might have been going on just prior to his death."

"Actually, the same thought occurred to me, so I've done some checking," Cody informed me. "I spoke to Glenda this morning."

Glenda was Mayor Bradley's secretary.

"And?" I asked.

"She said, off the record of course, that Bradley had been acting odd lately."

"Odd how?"

"For one thing, he'd been extrasecretive. Glenda said Mayor Bradley wasn't one to discuss his personal life in the office, but he never seemed to be hiding anything either. She shared that during the past two weeks Bradley had been closing the door between his office and hers the moment he arrived at work. In all the years she'd worked for him, she said Bradley never closed the door unless he was having a confidential conversation with someone."

"So what's been different the past couple of weeks?" I wondered.

"Exactly."

"Did Glenda say anything else?" I asked.

"Only that Bradley had begun keeping erratic hours. He was coming in late and staying late. She said she drove by his office one night last week and noticed the lights on at ten thirty. Glenda speculated that he might have been having marital problems. She said he normally was an eight-to-five kind of guy, but he'd followed a similar pattern a couple of years ago when he and his wife were going through a rough patch."

I stepped over a piece of driftwood that had washed up on the beach during the last storm. I really should move the thing. I'd tripped over it more than once during the past month.

"Did Glenda think the secrecy and the erratic hours were related?" I asked.

"She wasn't sure, but she did say that both behaviors began at about the same time. She also said Bradley had taken to locking the door to his office when he was out."

"So he was hiding something."

"It would seem that way. Glenda told me that she has a key to the office. She's had it for years. She wasn't sure if he forgot he'd given it to her or if he simply didn't care that she had access to his office."

"So he might have been locking the door to keep a specific person or persons out," I concluded.

"Most likely. Although, as Glenda indicated, he may just have forgotten she had the key."

Max ran over to me with a stick in his mouth. He had me trained well. As he'd taught me to do, I took the stick from him and tossed it into the waves. Max went charging after it with Rambler on his heels. The dogs really were having the best time together.

"Okay, so we know Mayor Bradley was acting strangely prior to his death, and that it was totally out of character for him to even set foot in the hollow, so what we need to find out is what caused his curious behavior and how that related to the hollow."

"In a nutshell. Glenda also mentioned the mayor had been receiving what she considered to be odd phone calls that he only answered on a burner phone she suspects he purchased for just that purpose."

"Did she know anything about the calls?"

"No. She said he received calls on the phone a few times when he was in the front office with her, but each time he immediately went into his office and closed the door."

"Does she happen to know where the phone is now?" I wondered.

"She said he always kept the phone in his pocket. I asked Finn if the phone had been found when the body was recovered and he said the mayor's pockets were completely empty with the exception of a black poker chip."

"A poker chip from where?"

"It was unmarked."

I frowned. There was something about the black poker chip that was nagging at a memory I couldn't quite grab hold of.

"He didn't even have his car keys or wallet on him?" I asked.

"Not according to Finn."

"Okay, that is odd." I stopped walking and looked at Cody. "In fact, now that I think about it, I realize it's strange that we didn't find Bradley's car near the entrance to the hollow. It's not all that close to his home or to town, so how did he get there?"

"Good question. I guess I should suggest to Finn that he track down the vehicle, if he hasn't already."

Max once again brought me the stick, and I once again dutifully threw it.

"I found Bradley's body on Monday during the late afternoon," I continued. "When Finn arrived at the scene he told me that it looked as if Bradley had been dead since early that morning. While Coffee Cat Books is closed on Mondays during the off season, the island offices are open. Mayor Bradley should have been in his office at the time he died. I wonder if he went in and then left, or if he never went in at all on Monday."

"That would be a good question for Glenda. I'll call her tomorrow. Do you think his attendance in the office that morning is relevant?"

"Maybe," I answered. "If he was in his office and then left to go to the hollow, he might have said something to Glenda before he left that could offer a clue."

Max returned with the stick and I took it from him again. "Okay, I'll throw it, but this is the last time. My arm is getting tired."

I threw the stick as hard as I could and Max set off after it. If you let him, Max would play fetch for hours.

"Did Finn mention how his interview with Bradley's wife went?" Cody asked after the dogs had gone for the stick.

"No. Once I mentioned Siobhan she was all he wanted to talk about."

Cody and I walked in silence for a spell. It was nice to feel Cody's big hand covering mine as the wind sent chills through my body. The sound of the water as it rolled in and out with the tide provided a soothing atmosphere with which to leave behind the stresses of the day.

"We should probably turn around," Cody suggested. "I'd like to get back to the house to spend some time with Mr. Parsons before he goes to bed. I've been so busy I've barely had any time to spend with him and I know he appreciates the company."

"That's fine. I have a busy day tomorrow, so I should have an early night anyway."

I called Max and Rambler as we turned and headed back down the beach toward my cabin. My place was small; really just a studio with a loft. But it was right on the beach, with some of the sweetest views in the area. It had originally been built as a summer cottage by Maggie's grandfather, but when Maggie realized how badly I wanted to move out of my mother's house, even though I had no money to do it, she'd offered to have the space converted into a year-round residence. It wasn't as insolated as it could be, and it had a tendency to be drafty in the winter, but it had a good wood-burning stove that kept Max and me toasty warm on most days.

"I noticed Destiny seemed a little down tonight," Cody said, changing the subject once we'd settled into our return trip.

"She had her appointment with the adoption agency. I think she's really conflicted. I hate to see her so stressed out, but I'm not sure how I can help her any more than I already have. I feel so helpless."

"You and Tara are doing a lot for her. I'm sure she appreciates it."

"She told me that Tara told her she could stay with her for as long as she wanted, even after the baby's born."

"That's generous of her."

"Tara is a generous person, and it seems like she's really bonded with Destiny. If she's able to stay with Tara at least until she finishes school, it might allow her to keep the baby."

"I guess it's good to have options."

I walked around a tree that had washed up onto the sand during the last storm. "I don't know. In a way I feel like the fact that she actually has options is making this even harder on her."

"It's a big decision." Cody squeezed my hand in what I could only assume was a gesture of comfort and support. "Any decision she makes is going to affect the rest of her life. Do you remember Tiffany Barstow?"

"Your huge seventh-grade crush. Yeah, I remember her."

"And do you remember she moved away when Danny and I were juniors?"

"Yeah. So?"

"The reason she moved wasn't because she decided to do a semester abroad, like she told everyone; it was because she was pregnant."

I stopped and looked at Cody. "Pregnant? Was the baby yours?"

"No. Tiffany and I were over by eighth grade and were just friends from that point forward. The point is, I ran into her a few years ago. She told me that she'd been sent away to live with an aunt until after the baby was born. She planned to have the child and then give it up for adoption so that no one on the island would know of her indiscretion. She even had a family picked out. Her aunt had arranged for the hospital to take the baby away as soon as it was born so she wouldn't have to see it and risk bonding with it."

"I guess that might be easier," I said.

"It probably would have been, but there was a storm the night the baby was born. The baby decided to come early, so there wasn't a plan to get her to the hospital. She was alone and the roads were closed."

"That must have been frightening."

"I'm sure it was terrifying. She delivered her baby on her own at her aunt's house while the storm raged outside. By the time medical personnel were able to make it through to her, she'd bonded with her daughter. Her name, coincidentally, is Destiny."

"She kept the baby?"

Cody nodded. "She's a beautiful little girl. Tiffany told me that keeping her daughter was the hardest decision she ever had to make. Her parents were so upset that they threatened to cut her off financially, and she almost changed her mind and went thought with the adoption at least a half a dozen times, but she stuck it out, and now she's very glad she did. She said her life wouldn't be the same if Destiny wasn't a part of it. In her own words, she and her daughter were destined to be together in spite of what anyone else might have thought about it."

"So you think our Destiny should keep her baby?" I asked.

"Not necessarily. I'm just saying that it's a big decision that will have a huge impact on the rest of her life, so she should take her time and be sure."

"Yeah, it really is a huge decision. She told me that she's going to go ahead and ask her doctor to tell her the sex of the baby. She didn't want to know at first, but she said it might weigh in to her decision."

"She has a preference?" Cody asked.

"She seemed to feel more confident about raising a girl on her own. She said a boy needs a dad, and she doesn't have any husband prospects, so she wasn't sure how she'd be able to fill that father role should she have a son."

"I guess that makes sense. It's nice when kids can have two parents, but in most cases boys do need a strong male role model more than girls do. Of course the role model doesn't have to be the boy's father. An uncle, grandfather, or family friend can usually fill in just fine. Besides, it seems like she might have something going on with Jake."

Jake was a boy Destiny went to school with who she spent a lot of time hanging out with, even now that she was no longer going to classes.

"She swears they're just friends, but I have a feeling they're just friends like we are," I commented.

Cody stopped walking. He turned and looked me in the eye. "And exactly how are we *just friends*?"

Me and my big mouth.

"You know." This was a conversation we needed to have at some point, but I wasn't certain this was the right time. Still, Siobhan had been right. If I didn't want someone else to scoop him up I'd best claim my territory. "I just meant that we're friends—good friends—who share common interests and values, and therefore we have the potential to, at some point, possibly, become something more."

Cody smiled. "Yeah."

I couldn't help but smile back. "Yeah."

"Would I be totally jumping the gun if I were to kiss you?" Cody leaned in so his lips were inches from mine.

"I think that might be okay." I closed the distance.

Chapter 4

Thursday, October 22

I woke the next morning to the sound of rain hitting the roof. Unfortunately, Cody hadn't been wrong about the bad weather, but I don't think even he realized it was going to arrive so soon. I rolled over onto my side and looked at Max, who had been sleeping next to me.

"Doesn't it seem like a perfect kind of day to pull the covers over our heads and go back to sleep?"

Max barked once. I couldn't help but notice the tone of judgment in his voice.

"I know I said I needed to get up early, but I was awake half the night. I really could use at least another hour."

Max just looked at me before he jumped off the bed, grabbed the covers with his teeth, and pulled them onto the floor.

"Okay, you pushy dog. I'll get up."

I'm not sure how Max knew which mornings I needed to get up and which I was actually able to sleep in. But somehow he knew the difference and always made sure I kept my commitments. Tara speculated that Max knew when I had set my alarm and when I had not and acted accordingly.

Still, having a dog for a warden did get aggravating at times, although as much as I hated to admit it, Max was right; I had promised Tara I'd be at work on time. Thursdays were shipment days and we always had a lot of unpacking and shelving to do before the customers arrived.

I pulled a knee-length sweatshirt over my head and stumbled down the stairs. Luckily, I'd thought to set the timer on the coffeepot the previous evening, and the rich aroma of coffee brewing was almost enough to give me the energy I so desperately needed.

I leaned against the counter as the brewing finished. I couldn't help but replay that one perfect kiss Cody and I had shared over and over in my mind. His lips had been both soft and firm and I could feel his heart pounding under my palm as I'd placed my hand on his chest. In actuality the kiss probably had been rather brief, but in my memory it went on and on. My heart told me that it had been so much more than just a kiss. I sensed that the moment our lips touched, our lives had touched as well, in a way I'd only dreamed of. Cody and I hadn't talked as he walked me back to the cabin. I don't think either of us wanted to ruin the moment with mindless chitchat. He kissed me on the cheek when we arrived at my door and wished me good night, but I could tell his heart held so much more.

I found that for the first time since those first days when he'd arrived on the island, I was actually nervous about seeing him. What if the kiss hadn't rocked his world the way it had mine? I felt like I'd been in this very situation ten years ago, when I'd seduced Cody on the eve of his leaving for his first tour in the Navy, and my sixteen-year-old heart had been certain he'd stay. But he hadn't. Of course back then he really had needed to leave. I just hoped my heart wouldn't be shattered again the way it had been back then.

Max barked to remind me that I'd forgotten to let him out. I crossed the room and opened the door, only to be greeted by an unexpected guest.

"I was wondering if you were going to show up at some point," I said to Ichabod, who was standing on the covered porch. I stepped aside so he could come in, which he did after hissing at Max.

"So are you here to help Finn, Cody, and me figure out who killed the mayor?" In my mind, the fact that Ichabod had shown up answered the question as to what had happened to Mayor Bradley. I doubted

Tansy would send a cat to help if Mayor Bradley had died as the result of an accident or suicide.

Ichabod jumped up onto the kitchen counter and began to meow. Apparently, he was more interested in breakfast than in conversation. I opened a can of cat food and spooned it into a bowl. I set the food on the mat next to the water dish and went in search of the litter box I'd used when my last kitty guest was in residence. So far the cats Tansy had sent to me only stayed until the murder they were sent to help with was solved. I missed the kitties that had come so briefly into my life, but I'd learned to accept the fact that they really were never mine to keep.

I was trying to decide what to make for breakfast when Max barked at the door to let me know he'd like to come back in. When I opened the door I noticed the light was on in Maggie's kitchen. I'd planned to stop by to check on Siobhan the previous evening, but the house had been dark by the time I'd arrived at the cabin. Deciding that breakfast could wait, I fed Max and then hurried upstairs to change into some warm clothing. After pulling my hair into a ponytail, I grabbed my coffee and an umbrella and headed to the main house.

"You're up early for someone who's on vacation," I commented to Siobhan, who looked gorgeous even though it was obvious she had been crying.

"I couldn't sleep. Is that coffee?"

"Yeah, but I only brought the one cup. I'll make a pot."

Siobhan smiled tiredly as I set to work measuring grounds and filling the water reservoir.

"Do you have any plans for today?" I asked.

"No. I thought I'd just hang out here."

"Does Mom know you're on the island?" I wondered.

"I hope not. I'm not sure I'm up to a visit from her quite yet. You haven't told her, have you?"

"No. The only people who know you're here, other than Tara, Destiny, and me, are Cody and Finn."

"You talked to Finn?"

"Yeah," I answered as I pulled a mug from the cupboard. "Remember, I told you that I was going to meet with him last night so we could discuss Mayor Bradley's death. You didn't say not to tell anyone that you were here, and I figured he'd want to know."

"How did he seem? Did he ask about me?"

"He was surprised to hear you were on the island, and I guess he was curious as to why you'd come home."

I poured Siobhan a cup of the freshly brewed coffee and then sat down at the table across from her. "Are you ready to tell me why you really are here?"

Siobhan looked at me with a tear in her eye. It was disconcerting to see my big sister looking so defeated. Siobhan had always been the strong one, who knew what she wanted and how to get it.

"What is it?" I placed my hand over hers.

"My life is a complete and total mess."

I waited for her to elaborate, but she didn't.

"In what way is your life a mess?" I finally asked.

"My boyfriend dumped me, I have no job, no car, and in a few days, no place to live."

"What? What happened?"

Siobhan looked up toward the ceiling, the way she did when we were growing up and she wanted to try to suppress the tears I knew were lurking just beyond her eyelids. I'm not sure when it started, but at some point Siobhan had decided it was a sign of weakness to shed a tear and she'd fought for control even when she had every reason to let go.

"Remember a couple of months ago I told you that the company I worked for had been sold and they were reorganizing?" Siobhan began.

"Yeah. You thought you were going to get a promotion and a raise."

"Well, I was wrong. I not only didn't get the promotion, but the job I've been doing better than anyone else for the past five years was eliminated."

"They fired you?" I asked.

"Technically they downsized me, but yeah, the end result is that I'm out of a job."

I tried to come up with something brilliant to say that would make Siobhan feel better, but I was coming up blank.

"I wasn't worried at first," Siobhan continued. "I have a strong résumé and a good reputation in the industry. I figured I'd get another job in no time. But I've been looking for two months and I've yet to get so much as a nibble. And then, to make matters worse, I wrecked my car and I can't afford to get it fixed, so I don't even have transportation to get to job interviews should I manage to actually get one."

"Wow. I'm so sorry. How can I help?" I asked.

"You can help me move. I have to be out of my condo by the end of the month. The rent is too high, and there's no way I can afford to stay where I am without a job. I've been looking for another place that's more reasonable, but apparently you have to have a job in order to rent an apartment. I have no idea what I'm going to do."

Siobhan lost her battle to prevent the tears she'd been suppressing from rolling down her face. I got up from where I'd been sitting and put my arms around my sister. I couldn't suppress my own tears as she sobbed into my shoulder. When it seemed she'd cried out all her tears, I handed her a tissue.

"Why don't you stay here?" I suggested. "With Maggie. Just until you can figure out your next move. You know she'd be happy to have you and she has a lot of extra bedrooms. We can put your stuff in storage while you look for a job and try to figure out what it is you want to do next."

"I really didn't want to come back to the island with my tail between my legs, but the reason I'm here is to ask Maggie if I can stay with her for a while. I hate asking for favors, but I really don't have a choice at this point."

I smiled. "I'm sorry you lost your job and your condo, but I'm happy you're home. Even if it is temporary. Everyone is going to be so happy to see you."

"Is Aiden back?"

"Yeah, he got back a few weeks ago."

Our oldest brother Aiden is a fisherman who had been in Alaska all summer.

"I guess I might call him to see if he can help me move my stuff into storage. Now that I've decided to come back to the island for a while I find I'm anxious to put Seattle behind me both literally and figuratively. The past couple of months have been horrible. I'm beginning to wonder why I ever thought I wanted to move there in the first place."

"Why *did* you move there in the first place?" I'd always wanted to ask her that, but I'd sensed she wouldn't have been receptive to my question.

"I don't know. Dad died and Mom and I were fighting all the time. My world felt so small, and I guess I was scared. Finn and I had been together forever and I really did love him, but I realized I wasn't ready to get married. I'd never lived anywhere but here and I never really dated anyone other than Finn. The more Mom and I fought over the wedding plans the more claustrophobic it began to feel. When I was offered the job in Seattle I jumped at the opportunity to run away and do something new.

Something on my own. It was the biggest mistake of my life."

"While the whole job thing didn't work out in the long run you learned a lot, made a ton of contacts, and really were successful. I wouldn't consider making the decision to take the job the biggest mistake of your life. You'll find something else eventually."

"That's not the mistake I was referring to."

"Finn?"

Siobhan didn't say anything, but I could tell by the look on her face that I'd hit it on the head. Siobhan was still in love with Finn. I knew he was still in love with Siobhan. Now all I had to do was to get those crazy kids together. I knew I'd need both a plan and reinforcements.

I looked at the clock on the wall. As much as I wanted to stay and chat with my big sister, it was getting late.

"I really do need to go. I have to see to the cats, take a shower, and get to the bookstore in less than ninety minutes."

"I can take care of the cats," Siobhan offered.

"Are you sure? I know cats really aren't your thing."

"I want to. It will give me something to do."

"If you want to drop me at work you can use my car today," I offered.

"Thanks, but I think I'll just hang out here and try to figure out what to do with my life. I might call Aiden. He's always a good one to talk to when you have a crisis."

"Yeah," I agreed. "He's the best."

"Is he still seeing Meghan?"

Meghan Halloway was Aiden's part-time girlfriend. He was away as often as he was home, so they'd never become serious, but when Aiden was on the island they tended to pair up.

"Yeah, she's been coming to Sunday dinner since Aiden has been back. It's nice to have a full house again. It's not like the huge meals we had when we were growing up, but most weeks Cody comes now that he's back, and Tara has been coming with Danny."

"Are Tara and Danny dating?" Siobhan looked shocked.

"I wouldn't say dating, but there's something going on. I think they've decided to take it slow, but I can tell they have feelings for each other that aren't of the friend variety."

"And Cassie?"

I laughed. "She has a boyfriend with tattoos, piercings, and colorful hair. He's a musician with a wide range of interests."

"I bet Mom hates that."

"Mom loves him," I countered. "Which I think makes Cassie love him less. You know how Cassie likes the bad boys. I honestly thought she'd dump him the minute she realized Mom loved the guy, but so far they're still together. You have to come to dinner this week. It'll be fun, and you can meet Cassie's guy."

"I might do that. I guess I'll see how the next few days go. I would like to see everyone, in spite of the fact that Mom will probably have me ready to pull my hair out by the end of the day."

"She's not that bad."

Siobhan raised one eyebrow.

"Okay, she can be a bit meddlesome, but she loves us and she means well. I really gotta go." I got up and turned toward the door. "I'll come by when I get home."

"Thanks, Cait. I really do feel better. I'm not sure how I totally missed it, but it seems my little sister is all grown up."

I grinned. It felt good to know I'd been able to help Siobhan for once; she'd been there for me so many times when we were growing up.

Chapter 5

I sat in my car when I first arrived at Coffee Cat Books, admiring the view. The rain had slowed to a drizzle, the hillsides were painted in fall color, and the ocean was dark with a mysterious feel. I'd strung orange lights around the doors and windows of the bookstore, and Tara had arrived early and turned them on. The window display Tara had taken so much trouble with brought an immediate feeling of Halloween to the deserted dock. I let the warmth and magic of the moment warm my heart before I headed into the store for the hectic day I knew was ahead.

"Oh, good, you made it on time," Tara greeted me as soon as I walked in the front door. "I wasn't sure you would because Siobhan is in town."

"I said I'd be here early and I am. I need to unload the cats, but I'll do whatever you need me to do after that."

I took the cats we featured in the cat lounge home each evening and brought them back in the morning. While they probably would have been fine if we left them overnight, I liked having them close by, where I could keep an eye on things.

"I've got half the shipment unloaded and inventoried, but I haven't had a chance to start stocking the shelves. Destiny is in the back entering the inventory into the computer. Once she does that we can start putting everything away."

"Give me a few minutes and then I'm on it. By the way, did Destiny ever hear back from her doctor?" I wondered.

"Not yet. He had some sort of an emergency yesterday. His nurse said he'd call this morning. I think Destiny is pretty nervous about the whole thing."

"Really. Why?"

Tara shrugged. "I don't know exactly. She didn't even want to know the sex of the baby at first, but now she seems to be of the mind that it could be the deciding factor in terms of her long-term plans. The thing is, I'm not sure if she's hoping it's a boy or a girl."

I frowned. "I don't get it. If she doesn't feel equipped to raise a boy on her own why would she be hoping for one?"

"It makes the decision for her about whether to pursue adoption, which will take a lot of pressure off. If it's a girl she still needs to decide what the best thing to do is."

When I gave it some thought I realized Tara's reasoning made sense. I couldn't help but feel for Destiny as I headed out into the drizzle to unload the four cats and two kittens I'd decided to bring. I'd thought momentarily about bringing Ichabod so we could start getting to know each other, but he's a beautiful black cat and I was afraid someone would want to adopt him. I'd learned along the way to let Tansy's cats set the pace, and when I'd left that morning Ichabod had been content to sleep by the fire. I had to wonder how he'd gotten to my cabin in the first place. The hollow was quite a ways from my home and it didn't seem likely he'd walked. Besides, it had been pouring rain all night. Maybe Tansy had dropped him off, or maybe he really was a magical kitty who had flown in on his magic kitty carpet.

"Everything is inventoried and ready to shelve," Destiny announced as I settled the last of the cats into the lounge.

"Perfect," I answered.

"I can help with the shelving if you don't have anything else you need me to do," Destiny offered.

"I don't want you lifting anything," Tara reminded her.

"I'm fine. I'm not even due for two months."

"I know, but we wouldn't want to hurt the baby. Why don't you start the book order we talked about yesterday?" Tara suggested.

Destiny shrugged. "Okay. I have the list we made in the back."

Destiny started toward the back room as her phone rang. She looked at the caller ID and hesitated. Finally, she lifted the phone to her ear.

"Hello?"

I couldn't help but watch Destiny's face as she listened to the person on the other end. She looked terrified, sad, and happy, all rolled into one.

"Okay, thank you."

Destiny hung up and looked to where Tara and I were standing.

"It's a boy."

I glanced at Tara. I had no idea how to respond. Should I congratulate her? Offer sympathy?

Tara didn't say anything; she just walked across the room and opened her arms. Destiny walked into them and began to cry. I suspected news of either sex would have been greeted with tears, but at least she now knew and could make her decision with all the information available to her.

"Are you open for business?" A woman walked in through the front door.

Destiny pulled away from Tara and headed down the hall.

"Did I interrupt something?" the woman apologized.

"You didn't interrupt anything and we aren't open quite yet, but I'd be happy to help you," Tara said. "Are you here for coffee or a book?"

"Both, actually."

I decided to start shelving the inventory while Tara waited on the woman. I considered going after Destiny, but my instinct told me that she needed some space to think things through. The poor girl had some tough choices to make in the weeks ahead. I'd noticed a difference in Destiny since she'd been living with Tara. She'd been an out-of-control teenager with a huge chip on her shoulder prior to becoming pregnant. After she found out about the baby she stopped sneaking out as often, but the chip on her shoulder had doubled in size. When I looked at her now, I saw a young woman with a good attitude who was mature and responsible. She had a job and was doing well with her homeschool lessons. In my opinion she just might be able to pull off single motherhood if she decided she wanted to try.

I paused to read the back of one of the books I was shelving. It was a mystery that took place in a small alpine town. The premise sounded intriguing. Maybe I'd give it a try if I ever again found the time to read. I didn't mind that my life was busy, but it did seem it was busier than was really manageable of late.

I looked up and watched as my favorite law enforcement officer walked through the front door. "Hey, Finn. You here for a cup of coffee?"

"Coffee sounds great, but what I really wanted was to talk to you. Do you have a minute?"

"Yeah, as soon as Tara finishes with her customer. I'll get your coffee and you can drink it while we chat."

By the time I poured Finn's coffee into a to-go cup, Tara's customer had left and Destiny had wandered back in. I suggested we talk in the cat lounge, which was occupied only by animals at the moment, so we could talk freely without worrying about being overheard.

"So do you have news about Mayor Bradley's death?" I asked when we were seated on one of the sofas.

"Not really. I still have no idea why he was in the hollow or whether his death was an accident or homicide. I've had a few leads I've explored, but I don't feel like I'm getting anywhere. The reason I'm here is to talk about Siobhan."

I guess I should have seen that coming.

"Do you know how long she's staying?" Finn asked.

"She didn't say specifically, but it looks like she's going to be here for an extended period. She's decided to take a break from Seattle, and as of this morning, she planned to stay with Maggie for a while."

"She's moving back?" Finn's dark eyes shone just a little bit brighter as the significance of what I'd said sank in.

"I wouldn't go so far as to say that, but she did indicate that she wanted to take some time to think about her future. My sense was that she would be on the island until she figured out what she wanted to do."

"So she left her job?"

"She's no longer with the firm she'd been working for," I confirmed. I didn't feel it was my place to tell Finn she'd been canned.

"Is she seeing anyone?"

"Not as far as I know," I answered honestly.

Finn sipped his coffee as he took a minute to process what I'd told him. I'd always suspected he'd never really gotten over Siobhan, but I didn't realize how totally into her he still was. I really hoped she wouldn't break his heart again.

"Do you think I should call her?" Finn asked.

Did I? I wasn't sure. Siobhan seemed to regret leaving him, but did that mean she was ready to pick up where she'd left off?

"Siobhan seems to need some time to herself at the moment," I answered. "I think she'll want to talk to you, but I'm not certain about the timing. Why don't you text her to let her know you'd like to get together for lunch when she has a chance? That way she knows you want to see her, but you're allowing her to set the pace."

"Okay. That sounds like a good idea. I'll do that."

"So about those leads that didn't go anywhere..." I said.

Finn looked at me. "I take it you think Mayor Bradley was pushed off that ledge."

"It's the only thing that makes sense, and even that doesn't make very much sense. Any way you slice it, the fact that Mayor Bradley was in the hollow, and on top of the cliff, doesn't jive with anything we know about him. For one thing, he hated cats. He'd never be hiking in the area for recreation, and if he wanted to kill himself he wouldn't do it surrounded by cats. At least I don't think he would. I guess you can never really know what a person is thinking. And besides the whole cat issue is the fact that it was a strenuous hike to the top of that bluff. I can't see Bradley making the climb unless he had a *very* compelling reason to do so. The guy was at least fifty pounds overweight and totally out of shape."

"So you're thinking someone somehow motivated Bradley to make the trip up to the bluff and then pushed him off?"

"That's my theory. Did you ever find Bradley's car?"

"No. It isn't at his home or his office. He either left it somewhere nearby and we simply haven't found it yet or the killer stole it, if there was indeed a killer. Chances are the killer left on the ferry, if that's in fact what happened, but I've been driving around looking for the car just in case."

"Mayor Bradley's car has a license plate that says 'Mayor B.' If someone stole the car and then took the ferry chances are the guys who work the car deck would have noticed. Have you asked around?"

"No, not yet, but that's a good idea. I suppose an intelligent killer would have traded out the plates, but you never know who might have wanted the man dead. It seems the idea that Bradley was murdered merits a bit more consideration than I originally thought."

"So like I said, about those leads?"

The first ferry of the day arrived shortly after Finn left. I watched as Wendy Pratt, a temp who worked for a variety of businesses around town, met a man in a dark suit. Wendy held an umbrella in one hand while she handed the man an envelope with the other. The man opened the envelope and pulled out a stack of papers. Then he said something to Wendy that caused a look of panic to cross her face. He looked at his watch as Wendy frantically looked down the street, as if trying to decide what to do.

I continued to watch as she took back one of the pieces of paper and then hurried across the dock toward the bookstore.

"Can I borrow your copy machine?" Wendy asked as she shook the rain from her umbrella.

"Sure. It's in the office."

She stowed her umbrella in the stand we had for that purpose and I led her down the hall. She put the paper down on the top of the machine and pressed the Copy button.

"Thank you so much. You're a lifesaver. I'm temping in Mr. Cloverdale's office this month and I would have been so fired if you hadn't helped me out. I was supposed to deliver some papers to a man on the ferry last week, but I totally spaced out on it, and he only comes on Thursdays, so I arranged to meet him today only to find out that one of the copies came out crooked and the signature line was cut off."

Talk about a run-on sentence.

"Luckily, Mr. Cloverdale has been out of the office for the past week and a half, so he doesn't know I screwed up. Hopefully, I can get this fixed before he finds out."

Wendy grabbed the copy she'd made and headed toward the door. "If I hurry I should be able to catch him before the ferry pulls out."

With that, she was gone.

"Was that Wendy?" Tara asked.

"Copy emergency."

Tara laughed. "She seems to have a lot of those."

"Wendy is supernice, but she's pretty disorganized. I'm not surprised she hasn't managed to land a permanent job."

Tara opened the top of the copier to refill the paper. "Oh, look. Wendy forgot her original."

"I'm going to meet Cody for lunch. Grover's office isn't too far from there; I'll drop it off." I slid the paper into my backpack. "I'd hate for Wendy to get fired."

By the time I joined Cody for lunch at the diner down the street the rain had stopped and the sky was beginning to clear, so I decided to walk the couple of blocks between the bookstore and the restaurant. I really enjoyed walking along Main Street during the holiday season. Almost all the shopkeepers went out of their way to create a festive atmosphere by decorating their windows and entries. The merchants all pitched in to buy white twinkle lights that were strung in all the trees along the main stretch of town. The lights gave the town a warm and inviting feeling from mid-October until after Presidents' Day.

"Most of what Finn shared with me really was useless," I told Cody after we'd been shown to our table. "But there are a few things I thought warrant a second look."

I tried not to stare at Cody's lips while we talked. I wasn't sure how things would be when we met for the first time after our amazing kiss, but Cody had just kissed me on the cheek like he always did, and he held my hand as we walked like he always did. I didn't exactly expect him to throw me to the ground and take me right there in the middle of Main Street, but I guess I expected *something* to be different. Maybe I should have suggested that he pick me up at the bookstore or that I meet him at the newspaper rather than at the diner, which was halfway in between.

"Such as?" Cody asked.

"Finn said he spoke to Nora Bradley. She claims she not only had no idea why he might have been in the hollow but she hadn't seen him for weeks. She confirmed that they've been having problems for a while and he'd moved out several weeks ago."

"Did she know where he was living?" Cody wondered.

"She told Finn she didn't know and didn't care. She was pretty sure he was having an affair, although she didn't have any proof. She filed for divorce last week."

"Normally, I'd say a cheating husband would provide a motive for the wife, but if she'd already filed for divorce chances are she was ready to move on, so there would be no reason for her to kill him unless she had a less than desirable prenup."

"Nora brought most of the money to the marriage," I informed Cody. "I doubt there was a prenup unless *she* wanted one to protect *her* money."

"It couldn't hurt to try to find out if the affair rumor is true, and if so, who he was having the affair with. Anything else?"

"Finn said he ran into Ty Poland, who mentioned that Bradley owed him a bunch of money for a dinner he catered a while back. Bradley was dragging his feet about paying him."

Ty Poland owned a local restaurant and had a sideline catering private affairs.

"Ty seemed to think the mayor was hurting financially," I added.

Cody frowned. "I suppose we can look into his finances. Did Finn say whether Ty went into any detail about the catering job, like who was in attendance or the purpose of the event?"

"Finn didn't say and I didn't think to ask. I'll follow up with him when I get a chance."

"Anything else?" Cody repeated.

"No, that's it. How about you? Do you have any new leads?"

"I spoke to Glenda again," Cody said. "She remembered that the mayor was supposed to meet with a man who wants to build a shopping mall on the island on Friday."

"Not that again." I groaned.

"Actually, Glenda said that when the man initially contacted him, he turned him down flat, citing the fiasco with Bill Powell as the reason. For some reason Glenda wasn't privy to, Bradley changed his mind and agreed to meet with the guy. When he came in to the office on Monday Glenda asked him how the meeting had gone, but he was vague and noncommittal."

"So did he work on Monday?"

"That was the other thing I was going to tell you. Glenda said he came in, went straight into his office, where he remained for a couple of hours, and then left, after stating that he wouldn't be back until the following day. She never saw him again."

"I sure would like to know what he was doing in his office."

"Glenda let me in and we took a look around."

"She let you into her boss's locked office?"

Cody smiled. "I can be very persuasive."

Yeah, you can.

"And?" I asked.

"I was hoping to find a flashing neon sign with our answer, but all we found were a few irregularities."

"What kind of irregularities?"

"Bradley's desk calendar indicated that he had a meeting the morning he died. It's unclear who the meeting was with."

"Did it indicate where he was to meet or what time?"

"He hadn't written down where he was going, but it did say 'TLB' in the ten o'clock slot."

"TLB?" I thought about it, but off hand I couldn't think of anyone with those initials. "If TLB stands for someone's name it could be a relative; the *B* could stand for Bradley."

"I'm not sure why you'd use all three initials of a person's name as a reminder, especially if they're a relative," Cody pointed out. "I was thinking it might stand for a name and a location. Such as Tom Lee at the beach or Ted Long at the Bayside Restaurant."

"Yeah, I guess that does make more sense. What else did you find?"

"There was a phone number jotted down on the calendar on the previous page. I tried calling it, and all I got was a recording stating the phone was no longer in service. I checked with a source at the phone company and was told the number belonged to an unregistered cell."

"You said Glenda mentioned he had a burner phone. Maybe it was his number."

"Maybe. At this point I'm not sure how that will help us."

"I guess there's not much to go on."

Cody shrugged.

We finished eating, and I hoped he would suggest that we spend some time together. I really couldn't get that one fantastic kiss off my mind. But instead of pulling me into his arms, Cody paid the bill like he always did, then took my elbow and walked me out the front door like he always did.

"I have some information back at the paper I'd like to discuss with you," Cody said as we paused on the sidewalk in front of the diner. "If you don't mind walking over with me I'll drive you back to the store so you aren't late."

I thought it odd that Cody was just now bringing up this information, but I shrugged and agreed to his plan. Cody's hand felt sweaty in mine as we walked the short distance to the building where Cody worked. If he were anyone else I probably would have simply let go, but holding Cody's sweaty hand was so much better than not holding his hand at all.

When we arrived at the newspaper Cody let us in through the front door. I noticed he didn't turn the "Be Back Soon" sign around, but maybe he didn't want us to be interrupted while we talked. He led me down the hall to his office and closed the door. Then he turned me so I was facing him and put his hands on either side of my face.

He looked deeply into my eyes and said, "I've been wanting to do this since I dropped you at your door last night."

His kiss was...well, *hot, hot, hot*. Unlike the kiss of the previous evening, which had been absolutely perfect if somewhat hesitant, the one today was possessive and powerful. I felt my body begin to shake as he awakened a longing deep inside me.

Eventually—much too soon, in my opinion— Cody stepped back. Then he pulled me into his body, wrapped his arms around me, and held me tight. I could hear his heart pounding against my ear, and if I never had to move again that would be fine with me.

"That was nice," I whispered.

Cody pulled back a bit and looked at me. He smiled. "Yeah. It was nice."

"Should we do it again?"

Cody groaned and took a full step backward. "I think maybe we'd better not. At least not now, when you have to go back to the bookstore and I have a paper to get out. Would you like to go to dinner tonight?"

I nodded.

"I was thinking we could try that new steakhouse on the harbor in Harthaven. I hear the food is excellent, and they have a huge menu if you aren't in the mood for steak."

I smiled. I realized that going to the steakhouse would require me to dig out a dress and appropriate shoes, but it seemed just right for my first date with Cody as a couple. At least I guessed we were officially a couple. "Maybe we can go back to my place after. We can build a fire and share a bottle of wine."

"Sounds perfect."

As soon as I arrived back at work I was informed that there was someone in the cat lounge who was interested in adopting one of the kittens I'd brought in with me that day. When I went in I saw Destiny talking to a little girl who looked to be five or six. The room was otherwise empty except for the cats.

"Tara said there was someone who was interested in adopting a kitten?"

"This is Amanda," Destiny introduced the girl with huge brown eyes and dark ringlets that reached her waist. "She'd like to adopt the white kitten you brought with you today."

"Wonderful." I looked around the empty room. "I'll need to have one of your parents fill out an application."

"My mom is in heaven," the girl announced.

"I'm so sorry." I closed the distance between us and sat down on the sofa next to the child.

"It's okay. She said God needed her to be an angel. I miss her, but she promised to visit me every night in my dreams and so far she has."

I felt my heart ache for this brave little girl. "Is your dad here, then?"

"No, he's at work. I came alone."

"You came alone? From where?"

"School. I know I shouldn't leave until it's over, but I wanted to find out about the kitten. My mom said I could have one."

"Your mom said you could have one before she went to heaven?" I asked.

"No. She said I could have one in my dream last night. The orange one is cute, but I want the white one. Angels are white."

"Yes, they are. Does your dad know you're here?"

"No. He wouldn't want me to have a kitten. He said we had enough troubles without adding an animal to the mix."

"I see."

I looked at Destiny. She shrugged. Apparently, neither Destiny nor Tara knew quite what to do with the motherless child, so they'd had her wait until I got back from lunch.

"I'm afraid I can't allow any of the kittens to be adopted unless a responsible adult fills out an application," I informed the girl.

"Oh." She hung her head sadly.

"How about if we go talk to your dad? I can't promise anything, but I would be willing to discuss the matter of your adopting a kitten with him."

The girl smiled. "Okay."

"You know that having an animal is a big responsibility."

"I know."

"And you'll have to promise to take care of her if your dad agrees."

"I will."

"Okay, let's go see what we can do. Where does your dad work?"

"At the market in Harthaven. His name is Mike."

"You're Mike Halloran's daughter?"

I'd heard that Mike's wife had died. He and I had gone to the same high school.

"Yes. He's my daddy."

I frowned. "Did you come all the way over here from the elementary school in Harthaven?"

"No. The one here. My daddy works in Harthaven, but we live here. We have a yellow house.

Yellow was my mommy's favorite color. She said it made her happy, like the sun."

"I like yellow also." I took the girl by the hand. "Let's go see what we can work out with your dad."

Chapter 6

"Do we really have to do this now?" I complained to Ichabod. I'd already showered and dressed in my skimpy red dress and the only heels I owned in preparation for my date with Cody when Ichabod decided he wanted to go outside and he wanted me to follow him.

I was behind schedule anyway, after spending a good part of the afternoon talking to Mike. In the end I was able to convince him to give adopting Angel a try. I promised to take the kitten back with no questions asked if it didn't work out, and I said I would spend some time with Amanda, showing her exactly how to take care of the young cat. Normally, I'm hesitant to adopt our cats into families where the adults weren't 100 percent committed, but Mike was a good guy who I'd known my whole life, and I was sure he'd be a responsible kitty parent whether he was enthusiastic about the adoption or not.

Besides, Amanda really got to me with those huge brown eyes and her insistence that her mom had told her it was okay to get a kitten. She even said it was her mom's idea to name her Angel. I spent at least an hour making sure Amanda had everything she needed to care for the cat and that she knew exactly what to do. I promised to visit them later in the week to make sure everything was okay.

"My feet are going to be filthy," I complained to Ichabod as I continued to follow him. I'd taken off my shoes so I could walk in the sand and I was tiptoeing around pieces of shell in my bare feet. "I'm going to have to wear tennis shoes with this dress if we don't go back right now."

The cat ignored me as he continued to walk down the beach toward a destination only he knew. At least the rain had stopped and the sky had cleared. There was still a chill and a dampness in the air that penetrated the thin material of my dress as if it weren't even there. No doubt about it, I wasn't dressed for beachcombing.

"I'm freezing," I muttered as I hurried to keep up with the cat. "What do you say we do this tomorrow?"

The cat continued down the beach past Francine Rivers's house. When he darted into the dense shrubbery that grew untamed near the intersection where the peninsula joined the main body of the island, I thought I'd lost him for sure. As I peered into the dense foliage, I heard a rustling just out of my sight.

"Ichabod?"

The cat meowed. I shoved the branches in front of me to the side, tearing my dress in the process. If this cat had brought me here to show me a dead seagull I was going to strangle him. Metaphorically. I would never actually injure the fur baby, no matter how aggravated I was with him. I gingerly stepped into the shrubbery, making my way slowly toward the spot where I heard Ichabod's cry. I stopped and screamed when my bare foot almost came into contact with the dead and bloated body of Grover Cloverdale.

I jumped backward and landed flat on my butt in the wet sand. Ichabod came over and licked my cheek as I tried to still my pounding heart. Unfortunately, I didn't have my phone with me, which meant I was going to have to run back to my cabin as fast as my bare feet would carry me to call Finn. Not that speed was of the essence. Grover was good and dead and there wasn't anything Finn or anyone else could do to change that. It looked as if he'd drowned, which was odd, because Grover couldn't swim and was terrified of water.

After I made it back to the cabin, I called both Finn and Cody, then headed upstairs to change into warm sweats. My fancy dinner with Cody would have to wait for another night. By the time I finished changing Cody had arrived, and he informed me that Finn had stopped by to let me know he was heading down the beach to retrieve the body.

By the time I'd poured myself a glass of wine Siobhan was poking her head through my side door.

"Did I see Finn's truck?" she asked.

"Yeah. Grover Cloverdale is dead. I stumbled across his body down the beach. Finn used our driveway to access the beach to retrieve him."

"Oh, God. What happened?" Siobhan shivered.

"It looks like he drowned." I handed my sister a glass of wine.

Siobhan frowned. "Grover hated the water. Why would he put himself in a situation where he would drown?"

"That was my first thought when I almost stepped on him."

I shuddered as an image of exactly what would have happened if I hadn't been able to stop myself and had actually stepped on him crossed my mind.

"I think I'm beginning to see a pattern," Cody said after he hugged Siobhan hello and opened the refrigerator in search of a beer. "Bradley hated cats, yet he died in the midst of hundreds of them, and Grover was terrified of water, yet he apparently drowned."

"Someone intentionally chose methods to kill those men that would feed on their greatest fear or biggest dislike," I concluded.

"It seems that way," Cody commented.

I opened the refrigerator and surveyed the contents. It was clear I wasn't going out for the fancy dinner I'd envisioned all afternoon. My refrigerator was so empty I was certain that if I spoke into it my words would echo. A trip to the market was definitely in order.

"It looks like Danny and Tara are here," Siobhan said as I closed the refrigerator door and began to peer through the cupboards.

I turned and watched as Siobhan put her wineglass on the table, then hurried out the door to throw herself into Danny's arms. Siobhan was born between Aiden and Danny and, in my opinion, had the closest relationship with both of them of any of the Hart siblings. There were times growing up when I was jealous of Siobhan and her easygoing relationship with both my big brothers, but today I was just happy she was here and smiling.

I watched as Danny twirled Siobhan in the air. Siobhan is small and petite like I am, but while my curly brown hair, sun-kissed skin, and smattering of freckles makes most people think of me as the girl next door, Siobhan is polished and sophisticated, with straight blond hair, sky blue eyes, and perfectly manicured finger- and toenails.

"It looks like they brought pizza," Cody said after Siobhan left the room.

"Good. I'm starving." I closed a cupboard door. "I'm sorry about our dinner. It looks like everyone plans to settle in for the evening."

"No problem," Cody answered. "We can do it another time."

Once everyone made their way back into the cabin, we all served ourselves a slice or two of the cheesy pie. I'm a pizza purist. If given the choice I will always request plain cheese or pepperoni. Tonight I was famished, so I selected one of each.

"You didn't bring Bandit?" I asked Tara about the kitten she usually brought with her when she came for a visit.

"He was all curled up with Destiny so I didn't disturb him. Jake is at the house, and the three of them are going to watch a movie."

"It seems like Jake has been around a lot," I commented.

"I encourage him to come by. He seems to have a way of cheering Destiny up when she starts to feel down. I really think he's good for her."

"He seems like a good kid."

"He's really mature and seems to know exactly how to deal with Destiny's mood swings. And he's smart too. One of the women who attend a pottery class with his mother told me that he wants to go to Harvard. Destiny hasn't always made the best choices as far as boyfriends go, but Jake seems like a keeper."

"I thought they were just friends," I said.

"They are. For now."

Maybe Jake and Destiny would find a way to take their relationship to the next level after the baby was born, the way Cody and I finally had. They really did seem to have a connection.

"Do you think Finn will come back by?" Siobhan asked when the conversation had died.

"I'm not sure," I answered. "I'm sure he'll want to talk to me at some point, but he'll need to make sure the body arrives at the morgue and that the next of kin are notified. I suppose it depends how long that all takes, but I kind of doubt he'll make it back here this evening."

I noticed Siobhan looked disappointed.

I smiled. Maybe Finn would be my brother after all. We continued to eat in silence for several minutes while the pizza was still hot. I was surprised to see that Ichabod was completely comfortable with the room full of people. Although I'd found him in the hollow, based on his friendly nature and the fact that he tolerated Max, I had to assume he came from a family with kids and other pets. I should really post a flyer in town to let people know I'd found him.

"Okay, so are we thinking that someone is out to eliminate the members of the Island Council?" Danny blurted out. Apparently, he was ready to move on from the topics of pregnant teens and ex boyfriends.

"It's the obvious link between the two men," Tara agreed.

"Oh, God, Maggie," I interjected.

"Maggie is off the island for another few days," Cody reminded me. "We just need to figure this out before then. I think I'm going to call Francine and Byron, though."

As of the recent Island Council election, there were five council members: Mayor Bradley, Grover Cloverdale, Francine Rivers, Byron Maxwell, and my aunt Maggie. Two of the five members had died under very strange circumstances in the past four days. If the motive behind the deaths of Bradley and Cloverdale was related to council business, both Francine and Byron could be in real danger.

"Francine is packing up Romeo and Juliet and coming to stay with Mr. Parsons, Rambler, and me until we figure this whole thing out," Cody announced when he returned from making his call.

I was glad to hear that because Francine lived alone with just her cats for company and protection.

"Byron said he'll be extracareful. His estate is gated and he has a security system, so as long as he's mindful of his surroundings when he's away from home he should be okay," Cody added.

"Neither of the two men appeared to have been shot, so whoever killed Bradley and Grover must be known to them," I said. "It seems like in both cases the killer must have gotten up close and personal."

"How did Grover end up in the water?" Tara wondered.

"We don't know yet, but Finn speculated that, based on where he was found, he was most likely pushed from a boat. That makes the most sense unless you take into account the fact that Grover would never have voluntarily gotten onto a boat in the first place," I answered.

"Any more than Bradley would have gone to the hollow," Tara added.

"I'm beginning to think that being elected to the Island Council comes with an expiration date," Danny commented.

I knew he meant that in terms of life expectancy rather than the length of the term the council members served. First councilman Keith Weaver had been killed, although it turned out the reason for his demise had had nothing to do with his role on the council, and then another councilman had been removed after he fell victim to a blackmail scheme.

"So where do we start?" Danny asked.

"I guess we should look at what's going on with the council that might create a motive for someone to want members dead," I offered.

"We need a murder board," Siobhan announced.

"A murder board?" I asked.

"Yeah, you know, like in the movies. We can list both men and their connections to each other, as well as anyone who might want them dead."

"I don't have a board to use," I said.

Siobhan stood up. "Maggie has that huge whiteboard in the sewing room." She looked at Danny. "Help me get it."

Danny shrugged, stood up, and followed her out the door. Siobhan always had been the type to take charge. I had a feeling our group had a new leader. She really would make a good wife for Finn. She could keep him organized and help him solve crimes. Of course I really didn't see her doing the actual investigating the way Cody and I often did. Siobhan didn't like to get her hands dirty. She was more of an idea person.

Danny and Siobhan returned with the whiteboard, colored markers, and sticky notes that could be moved around the board easily.

"Okay, who wants to start?" Siobhan asked once everything was set up.

"Glenda did say Bradley met with a developer who wants to build a shopping mall on the island," Cody began.

"A shopping mall?" Siobhan smiled. "I don't see how that's a motive for murder, but I will say I'm glad to hear it. It's about time this island finds a way to attract decent shopping."

"Not everyone feels the way you do," I explained to Siobhan. "There are a lot of residents who think a large development will ruin our island charm." I briefly explained all the fallout caused by Bill Powell's condo project.

"So no mall?" Siobhan looked disappointed.

"Hopefully not," I answered. "Glenda said that initially Bradley was dead set against the project, but then something happened to cause him to change his mind. At least she *thinks* he changed his mind. All Glenda knew for certain was that Bradley met with the man on Friday. She didn't know the outcome of their discussion."

"Sounds like a motive for murder to me," Tara said.

Siobhan wrote the words *mall project* under Bradley's name. She'd drawn a line down the middle of the board and written Bradley on one half, Grover on the other. She then set up two columns under each name that said *motives* and *suspects*. She really did have the gift of organization.

"It seems like the mall project is worth looking in to, but I don't think we should focus on that to the exclusion of everything else," Danny commented. "What else is the council working on?"

"I overheard Mr. Parsons and Francine talking about the local parcel tax to help fund the schools that some of the residents are supporting," Cody said. "I'm not sure how that would get someone killed, but according to Francine there's a lot of controversy among the island's residents."

"No one wants a new tax," I supposed.

"True. I doubt that there's a single person on the island who's excited about having to pay more taxes, but the parents of many of the younger kids are pushing for upgrades to the infrastructure of the school building and the addition of a computer lab," Cody informed us. "Plus there's the fact that overall enrollment is down, which means less money coming in from the state."

"Why is enrollment down?" Siobhan asked.

"A lot of families left the island when the cannery closed, and many of their houses were bought by people from the mainland looking for vacation homes after the ferry began docking here. Fewer resident children means less money to pay teachers and improve schools."

I hadn't really stopped to consider how the changing economy would affect things like schools. Cody made a good point about the tax, but I couldn't see someone killing anyone over it. The tax, while unwelcome, wouldn't be a life-changer for the average person.

Siobhan went ahead and created a column that represented motives that applied to both men. Then she jotted down the word *tax* with a question mark.

Cody mentioned a few other things he knew were on the agenda for the next council meeting, but none of them appeared to be items anyone would care enough about to kill someone over. The point that was nagging at my mind as we discussed hot-button issues was that the murders seemed personal. If someone wanted to kill council members in order to influence the outcome of a piece of legislation before the council, why go to all the trouble of drowning Grover or killing Bradley in the presence of cats?

"So what else do we have besides council business?" Siobhan asked.

I shared the fact that Bradley was supposedly having an affair and that his wife had filed for a divorce. I also mentioned he'd been extrasecretive as of late and that there was a rumor he was in financial trouble.

I thought about the fact that Grover had sold a large piece of land to a local developer not long ago. The only reason I knew this was because the land had been in the middle of the Bill Powell scandal. I hadn't stopped at the time to consider why Grover would have sold the land, which had been in his family for generations, but Glenda had told Cody that Bradley seemed to be having financial issues, so I had to wonder if Grover wasn't having money problems as well.

"Maybe we should look into Grover's finances," I suggested.

"That's a good idea. And I'll talk to Francine to see if she has any other input on what the council might be up to," Cody offered. "I'll also talk to the island clerk to see if I can get hold of the next agenda. While I'm at it I can see if there've been any applications for new businesses or developments submitted lately that could lead to a motive."

That made sense because Francine was going to be staying temporarily in the house he lived in with Mr. Parsons.

"I'll have a chat with my neighbor Lacy," Tara offered. "She cleans the Cloverdales' house."

I knew who Lacy was. She cleaned the homes of several of the area's longtime residents. She was also a conservationist who was almost radical in her mission to save the area's undeveloped spaces. A lot of the island's residents referred to her as tree-hugger, but as far as I could tell she was a nice woman and a good worker. I knew Maggie had hired her to clean her house a time or two and had been pleased with the results.

"I'm betting that if Grover was feeling stressed over something she'd know about it. She lurks better than anyone I know, plus she's a snoop," Tara said.

"A snoop?" I asked.

"She likes to dust inside drawers, closets, and file cabinets."

I frowned. Maybe I should mention that to Maggie.

"Don't worry; she's a snoop but not a gossip. I don't think she spreads around what she knows."

Siobhan wrote Lacy's name down on the whiteboard.

"Okay, what else?" Siobhan asked.

"I can head over to the Fisherman's Lodge to see if anyone knows what might have been going on in the private lives of both men," Danny offered. "They were both regulars."

The Fisherman's Lodge is a club of sorts for the men on the island. To belong to it you must be male—which has caused quite a bit of angst among the female population—and you must either be a member of the fishing industry or a descendant of a member of it. Grover was a mostly retired attorney and Bradley was the mayor, but both of their grandfathers had fished for a living.

"What can I do?" Siobhan asked. "I want to help."

"There's a new manager at the bank," I said.

"Yeah, so?"

"How would you like to help me sweet-talk some information out of him?"

Siobhan smiled. "I can do that."

Chapter 7

Friday, October 23

    Friday dawned bright and sunny, although the weather forecast called for rain by evening. My plan was to get up early, take Max for a run, care for the cats in the sanctuary, arrive at the bookstore on time, work until lunch, and then pick up Siobhan so we could pay a visit to our local bank. I was proud of myself when I got out of bed before the alarm sounded and without Max's prodding. I dressed in warm layers, pulled my knit hat onto my head, and was heading toward the side door when Ichabod made it clear my plans were not necessarily his.

"You're kidding, right?" I asked the cat as he dashed out the door and into the bright sunshine. "Can't whatever it is you have for me to find wait? I haven't had a chance to take Max for a run for several days."

The cat began to walk in the direction in which he'd taken me when I'd found Grover's body. I was glad I knew Francine was safe at Mr. Parsons's. I would have been worried sick as we headed toward her property if I didn't know for certain she and the cats were with Cody.

As I continued to follow Ichabod, I let my mind wander. Max was having a good time romping in the waves and I had my tennis shoes on this time because I'd planned to go out for a run. Ichabod was taking me toward the same spot we'd gone the last time and I wondered if the poor thing was confused and didn't realize we'd already found the body in the water.

The conversation I'd had with the gang last evening had left me sleepless for a good part of the night. Everyone had shared important theories and information, but I found I couldn't imagine how it all might fit together. Or even if it *did* fit together. The fact that two of our Island Council members had turned up dead within days of each other seemed to indicate it was island business that had led to their demise, but had it? I remembered Keith Weaver's death and the certainty with which I'd felt it was his role on the council that had led to his early demise, when in reality it was something else altogether. It seemed it was best to keep an open mind.

When we came to the place where I'd found Grover's body, Ichabod veered toward the water. Suddenly I began to dread what I would find at the end of the trail. Certainly not another body…

I walked carefully through the foliage until Ichabod stopped. Lying in the sand, which had been revealed by the low tide, was a black poker chip, just like, I imagine, the one found in Mayor Bradley's pocket.

I called Finn because I was certain he'd want to know, and then Cody because I wanted an excuse to talk to him before I became busy with the demands of the day. We hadn't had a minute alone together since our kiss in his office and I was dying to see what came next for us.

While neither of us had ever professed our love for each other, I felt he'd shown me how he felt by the little things he did for me. He took Max to work with him most days so my best buddy wouldn't have to be alone. On the days he couldn't take him, he picked him up and took him over to Mr. Parsons's.

A couple of weeks ago I'd come home from work to find a half gallon of milk in my refrigerator. When I mentioned it to Cody, he'd said he'd noticed I was low and realized I was busy, so he'd picked some up so I wouldn't have to drink my coffee black.

I knew Cody would fit right into my family should we decide to become serious about each other. He'd been best friends with Danny his entire life and he got along with Aiden, Siobhan, and Cassidy as well. He came to Sunday dinner with me every week, even when it meant he'd miss watching a big game on TV. And while he was at my mom's, he went out of his way to charm her into loving him like a son.

I got Cody on the phone and he said he'd be right over, and Finn assured me he'd be at the cabin within a half hour. So much for getting to work early. I called Tara and explained what had happened and that I might very well be late. It was a good thing Tara was so easygoing. It seemed that for one reason or another I was late for work quite a lot.

"So what did Finn make of the fact that both our victims were found with black poker chips?" Tara asked when I finally managed to make it to Coffee Cat Books.

"He seemed to think the black chips were meant to serve as a signature of some sort," I answered as I tied the pink apron with the Coffee Cat Books logo around my waist.

"Signature? That sounds like a serial-killer thing."

"Yeah. Unfortunately, it does, although based on the way the men died I'm going to put my money on the killer being someone who knew the men. Probably someone who knew them well."

"That's disturbing." Tara frowned.

"When I saw the chip the image of a black rose flashed through my mind. Didn't we read a book a while back where the killer left a black rose lying across the chest of each of his victims?" I decided I really could use a latte after the morning I'd had, so I began to gather the items I'd need.

"Yeah. We read it in book club several years ago. But I see your point. Maybe the killer puts a black chip into the pocket of each of his victims. Bradley's chip was found in his pocket and Grover's was found near where the body was recovered. It could have fallen out of his pocket when they moved his body. I'm beginning to feel a little uneasy about all the unanswered questions. Francine moved over to Mr. Parsons's house so she wouldn't be alone, which made perfect sense because she's a member of the Island Council, but what if the killer just chose two victims at random who just happened to both be councilmen?"

"I think the likelihood of that is pretty slim, but maybe you and Destiny should move over to Maggie's house for a few days," I suggested as I took a sip of my drink. "She has eight bedrooms all made up and ready for guests. I don't necessarily feel any of us would be targeted, but we are snooping around and the killer may realize that. I'm sure Siobhan won't mind the company, and Maggie won't be home until Sunday night. I can ask Danny if he's willing to stay at the house as well. There's safety in numbers."

"I guess I would feel better having other people around, and I do hate to leave Destiny alone for any length of time."

"Then it's settled. Pack a bag and come over after work. Where is Destiny anyway?"

"She had a doctor's appointment and then she was going to head over to St. Patrick's to work on her lessons," Tara informed me. "She said she'd come in this afternoon and finish the bookkeeping she started yesterday."

"She really is catching on to that."

"She is. I know we hired her as a means of helping her out, but it's worked out that she's actually helping us. I hope she'll be willing to stay on after the baby is born."

"Has she said anything more about her plans for the baby now that she knows it's a boy?" I asked.

"No. But I can tell she's thinking about it. I don't think having a boy is the obstacle she initially thought it would be. I know she's discussed her situation with Jake, although I'm not sure where he stands on the whole keep-the-baby/don't-keep-the-baby debate."

"My heart aches for her every time I think about what she's going through."

"Yeah, mine too. Despite the fact that we're doing all we can to help her, I'm sure she feels pretty alone."

"And I'm sure it's hard on her not to have her mother's support," I agreed.

The conversation paused when two women came in and ordered pumpkin lattes. It had been Tara's idea to feature a different specialty each month at a discounted price, and so far the idea had paid off in spades. Most customers wanted a muffin or scone to go with their beverage, so although the coffee was discounted we ended up making a nice profit on each order.

"By the way, I forgot to tell you that I called Lacy this morning," Tara said after the women left.

"And?" I asked.

"And there was definitely something going on. Lacy said Grover had cut back her hours a while back after telling her that he needed to deal with some financial problems."

"So Bradley and Grover both had financial concerns. Do you think they were gambling?"

Tara frowned. "I guess they could have been. They were both found with a poker chip and they were both suffering from a financial shortfall. You should definitely mention that to Finn."

"I will. Did Lacy say anything else?"

"She said that, like Bradley, Grover and his wife were having marital issues. Lacy thought it was due to the strain the money problems had put on the marriage, but she couldn't be sure. She did say that Grover had been sleeping in the guest room for months."

I'd been certain the men were killed as a result of their position on the Island Council, but now I wasn't so sure. It seemed just a bit too coincidental that both men were having financial and marital issues.

"The only other thing she mentioned was that she'd overheard Grover arguing with one of the men who hang out at the lodge. She seemed to think the answer to the question of who killed the men most likely would be found among the fishermen who frequented the place."

I frowned. "Really? That seems like a long shot to me."

"I'm just sharing what she said. I have to agree with you, though. I don't see any of the guys from the lodge as being the sort to kill two men in cold blood."

"I don't know," I countered. "A couple of those guys are downright scary."

Our conversation was interrupted when the noon ferry arrived. Although our business tended to be slower now that summer was over, Fridays were as busy as ever because tourists from the mainland still came in droves for the weekend. I was supposed to pick Siobhan up at three so we could go to the bank, so our chat would have to be put on hold until later that evening.

"Is that what you're going to wear?" Siobhan asked me when I went by Maggie's to pick her up for our afternoon of sleuthing.

I looked down at my jeans and pink Coffee Cat Books T-shirt. "What's wrong with it?"

Granted, Siobhan looked elegant and sophisticated in her dark brown slacks, matching heels, and burnt orange sweater. Her blond hair hung perfectly straight to her waist and her makeup had been applied expertly, giving her a polished look, while I looked somewhat less pulled together. Still, we were going to be sleuthing at the local bank, not attending a fancy seminar in the city.

"If you're going to ask a man you've never met to invest in your idea you're going to need to look the part," Siobhan argued.

"What man and what investment? We're going to the bank to dig up some dirt on Mayor Bradley and Grover Cloverdale, not take out a loan."

Siobhan took me by the hand and led me up to the bedroom she'd been using. "You can't just waltz into the bank and ask for information on them straight out. You need a reason to be there, thus the loan."

Once we arrived in her room she opened the closet and began sorting through the contents.

"But I don't need a loan," I argued.

"The loan isn't for you personally; it's for the bookstore."

"But we already have a loan."

Siobhan tossed me a pair of camel-colored slacks and told me to put them on. While I changed she looked for something to replace my T-shirt.

"The loan is for your expansion," Siobhan informed me.

"Expansion? What expansion? We only just opened a few months ago. We don't need to expand. More importantly, we can't afford to expand."

Siobhan tossed me a sage green sweater and then began sorting through her shoes.

"The bookstore is great. It really is. I just think that if you really want to make a go of it you'll need to expand your Internet presence. Internet retail is the wave of the future. And the present, for that matter."

I pulled the sweater over my head. Although Siobhan and I wore the same size we'd never shared clothes before, due mainly, I imagine, to the fact that we had very different tastes.

"The charm of the island is our niche," I explained. "People come to our store because they want to buy a book at a cute little shop on the harbor. I doubt we'd sell very many books over the Internet. Not only is there an inventory issue but the postage would make it difficult for us to make a profit."

"I'm not talking about paperbacks, I'm talking e-books and audiobooks."

"We don't carry e-books and audiobooks," I pointed out.

"Exactly. Try these shoes on, but wash your feet first."

"I took a shower this morning."

Siobhan looked down at my dirty tennis shoes. I washed my feet.

"Look, while I think your business is ripe for expansion, I'm not really trying to have you borrow money at this point. The loan simply gets us in the door. Once we have a reason to take up the bank manager's time we can slip in the questions we really want to ask."

"I think you might need an appointment for something like that," I pointed out as Siobhan brushed out my hair and then pulled it back with a wide clip.

"I called this morning and made one. If anyone asks, I'm your business consultant. Maybe just a tiny bit of makeup. Have a seat on the bed."

I sat down while Siobhan finished cleaning me up. Not that I was dirty. Exactly. I have to admit that between the cats and Max, I have some amount of pet hair on my clothes 24/7.

Siobhan stepped back. "There. That should do it. You look beautiful."

I glanced in the mirror. I'm not sure I'd use the word *beautiful*, but I did look different. I wouldn't want to try to maintain this look every day, but I actually looked like I belonged in a business meeting.

"I think we're ready," Siobhan announced. "Now remember, let me do the talking. I'm used to negotiating business deals, so I know what I'm doing."

"But we don't actually want a loan," I reminded her.

"For now. But it doesn't hurt to put the idea out there. I called Danny to come by and pick us up. Your car is covered in cat hair."

By the time we made it out to the front drive Danny was waiting. I couldn't help but feel like the little sister; Danny and Siobhan sat in the front and chatted and I sat in the back in silent isolation. I loved

Siobhan, and I was very happy she'd come home to the island, but I wasn't sure how I felt about being relegated to the backseat both figuratively and literally.

I will admit Siobhan hadn't been wrong about dressing the part. After arriving at the bank we were offered a beverage and then immediately shown into the new bank manager's office. It took less than ten minutes for my sister to have the man completely wrapped around her little finger. I still wasn't sure expanding the bookstore was something we should be considering, and I could never make such a decision without Tara, but if we ever did find ourselves in need of a loan, hiring Siobhan to negotiate the deal wouldn't be a bad idea. Not only was she beautiful but she was intelligent, articulate, and had a presence that couldn't be ignored. The company she'd worked for must have been insane to let her go.

"We totally rocked that meeting," I said to Siobhan as we were leaving the bank. Not only did Coffee Cat Books have a tentative offer of a loan to expand into e-distribution should we decide to go ahead with the idea but we'd learned some interesting facts about both Mayor Bradley and Grover Cloverdale as well.

"It's all in your approach," Siobhan informed me. "You have to own the meeting from the moment you walk into any negotiation. It looks like Finn is talking to Danny."

I looked toward the parking lot. Danny was standing next to his car waiting for us and Finn had pulled up next to him in his sheriff's department vehicle.

"Do I look okay?" Siobhan asked.

Suddenly, my self-confident sister looked like a scared little girl.

I took Siobhan's hand in mine and gave it a squeeze. "You look beautiful."

"I'm so nervous."

"It's just Finn," I reminded her.

"What if he hates me now?"

"He doesn't hate you."

Even if he had every reason to, as far as I could tell he was still totally in love with my big sister.

"They noticed us," I informed Siobhan. "Danny is waving us over."

"I can't." Siobhan stood perfectly still.

"Just take a step forward," I coached.

I began to walk toward the parked vehicles with Siobhan at my side.

"And smile."

Siobhan did.

I looked at her. "And breathe."

Siobhan stopped walking. She looked at me and laughed. "You want me to walk and smile *and* breathe?"

I laughed back. "I guess that *is* a lot."

Siobhan let out a long breath. "I'm ready. Let's do this."

Chapter 8

Later that evening Cody, Tara, Danny, Finn, Siobhan, and I, met at the cabin to continue the investigation. Once Siobhan and Finn got past that first awkward greeting, I could see that things were going to be fine. They'd always been friends and I could see that a broken engagement wasn't going to change that.

I was happy to have Finn and Siobhan talking again, but there was no doubt about it: Siobhan and her murder board had taken over the leadership of the sleuthing gang of which I'd previously been the director. I guess I shouldn't be surprised. Siobhan was the type who liked to drive the bus. And she was good at it. She managed to demand everyone's attention as she systematically added new clues to the whiteboard and deleted others.

"What did you find out at the lodge?" Siobhan asked Danny.

"Both men were active members and had been there within a week of their deaths. I was able to confirm that both Bradley and Grover were regulars in the backroom poker game that's held among members who are invited to take part."

"Have you ever played?" I asked.

"No. I don't hang out at the lodge all that much. I'm a member by birth and profession, but I rarely attend any of the meetings or events. Most of the guys who spend time there are old enough to be my grandfather. And I've never participated in the poker games; too rich for my blood. Most of the men who participate come from old money. To be honest, the old farts who play really don't welcome newcomers even if they have money. They're pretty set in their ways."

"But you know who does play," Tara coaxed.

"Sure. I guess."

Siobhan got up and flipped the whiteboard over to the other side. She started a new list, beginning with Mayor Bradley and Grover Cloverdale.

"Okay, who else participates in the gambling?" She looked directly at Danny.

"Buzz Walton, for one."

Buzz was a crusty old fisherman with salty stories and a crabby disposition, but he'd always seemed like a nice enough sort.

"And Leif Piney, for another."

Leif was a retired fisherman who was around seventy. He was equally as crusty as Buzz but not as well liked. Leif was a rugged man who didn't have much use for women, children, or anyone under forty and wasn't afraid to let you know it.

"Jasper Colton, Frank Dakota, and Brian Quinn."

All were retired fishermen in their sixties or seventies, and all had lived on the island their entire lives.

"Dad was a regular before he passed, and Aiden sometimes takes his place when he's in town," Danny added.

"Aiden? Really?"

Aiden was about as straitlaced as they came.

"I think he does it more for the sense of tradition than anything else."

"Are there ever any new men allowed to join?" Tara asked.

"When I was at the lodge checking things out today, I found out that a couple of months ago a man from out of the area requested membership. He was a stranger to the island, but he claimed to be a fisherman by trade and he was male, so technically they had no reason to keep him out. He was a likable enough fella named Jeremy Vance. They couldn't keep him out, but most of the guys refused to accept him no matter how hard he tried to fit in. Personally, based on the stories the men from the lodge told me, I think it was because he was good at poker and was single-handedly responsible for the financial decline of several of the good old boys."

"Do you think he was cheating?"

"I don't know if he was cheating or not, but the guys were sure he was. I guess they managed to find a way to get rid of him because as far as I heard he doesn't come around anymore."

Siobhan had written everyone's name on the board as Danny mentioned them. When she was done she took a step back. "I don't know what any of this means, and while I've been away for a few years now, I can't believe any of these men would kill Mayor Bradley or Grover."

"What about this Jeremy Vance?" I asked. "You said the guys managed to get rid of him. Maybe he was mad enough about being kicked out of the club to take revenge on the men who refused to accept him."

"It seems like a long shot," Finn commented.

"Yeah, we might be barking up the wrong tree with the poker angle," I commented. "It still looks like the common link is the Island Council, although Lacy seemed to think we'd find the killer among the men who hang out at the lodge."

Siobhan moved around a few of her sticky notes and added a few others.

"Why did Lacy think that?" Finn asked.

"She said she overheard Grover arguing with one of the men; she wasn't sure who. She seemed to think there was tension within the ranks of the good old boys."

Finn frowned but didn't say anything.

"Okay. Cody, why don't you tell us what you found out from Francine concerning the mall project?" Siobhan directed.

"While it may or may not have been true that Mayor Bradley met with the developer who wanted to build the mall, Francine said the development of the project was never going to pass the council and everyone knew it. When the developer first brought his idea forward, he was told he would be best served by looking for another location. Francine is of the opinion that even if the developer had managed to change Bradley's mind, it wouldn't have done any good because the other four members of the council were dead set against it."

"In other words, unless this developer was willing to kill all five council members there was really no way he was going to get a permit to do what he wanted to do," Danny contributed.

"Two of the five are dead," Tara pointed out.

"While that's true, I think killing two people in order to build a mall is a long shot," I countered. "There has to be an easier way to make a buck."

"I agree with Cait," Siobhan spoke up. "We found out at the bank today that both Bradley and Grover were on the verge of bankruptcy. If this developer really wanted to build his mall all he had to do was bribe them. Killing them makes no sense. I think we can eliminate the developer as a key suspect." Siobhan looked at Finn. "Do you agree?"

"Actually, I do," Finn answered. "I've done some checking and apparently, the developer has already applied for a permit to build on the Olympic Peninsula. I don't see a monetary reason for him to have killed two men, and as far as I know, he didn't have a personal relationship with either of them. I think we can eliminate him as a suspect."

Siobhan erased the developer's name but started a new column on the side of the whiteboard: *eliminated suspects*. It was a smart thing to do, in case we needed to come back to them for any reason.

"Anything else?" Siobhan asked Cody.

He nodded. "While Francine didn't feel the mall was a motivation for murder, she did think there was another issue that was worth looking at. It seems Mayor Bradley wanted to remove the cats from the hollow."

"What? Why?" I asked.

Cody shrugged. "You know Bradley. As far as he was concerned, all cats are evil. He planned to hire a service to relocate them."

"That's crazy," I spat. "Why didn't Maggie say anything?"

"Francine thinks she didn't want to worry you."

I frowned. I guess it made sense that she would want to protect me. "Relocate the cats to where?" I asked.

Cody shrugged. "Francine didn't know. She suspected they planned to exterminate them once they'd removed them. Glenda was also sure that was the intention of the company Bradley was talking to."

"Could he have done that?" Tara asked.

"I'm afraid so," Cody answered. "It turns out the land where the hollow sits is owned by Nora Bradley."

"Do you think Nora knew what her husband planned?" I asked.

"Nora isn't an animal rights activist, but I don't see her agreeing to a plan that includes killing a whole lot of cats," Tara put forth.

"I agree with you. I'm not sure how Bradley planned to pull that off, but I'm betting Nora didn't know anything about it. Someone needs to stop him," I exclaimed.

"Someone did," Siobhan pointed out.

Siobhan was right of course. Someone *had* stopped Mayor Bradley. With him out of the way the whole plan would die.

"I guess it's a good thing Maggie is away at her yoga retreat," I joked. "If she were here she'd be the number-one suspect."

"There is no yoga retreat," Finn informed me. "I checked, and the retreat Maggie claimed she left the island to attend was held two weeks ago."

"Surely you don't think Maggie did this?" Siobhan accused.

"I hope she didn't. I don't want to think her capable of such an act. But she had motive and I can't find evidence that she ever left the island. I've talked to everyone who works the car deck on the ferry and no one remembers seeing her on it."

"A lot of cars take the ferry," Tara insisted.

"True, but everyone knows Maggie," Finn reminded her. "She always stops to chat with whoever's working. I confirmed that John and the regular crew were working on the day she told everyone she was leaving. They would have recognized her car."

"You can't seriously be suggesting that Maggie killed these men?" I asked.

"If she isn't guilty and she isn't at the retreat, where is she?" Finn asked.

I looked at Cody. I could tell he'd had the same thought I had. I really hoped Maggie hadn't been our killer's third victim.

Cody stayed to make sure I was going to be okay after Finn went home and Siobhan, Danny, and Tara all headed to Maggie's house for the night. They'd tried to convince me to go up to the big house with them, but I needed to be alone with my thoughts.

There was no way Maggie would kill anyone, yet I had to admit that when Cody had told us Bradley's plan, thoughts of murder were very much on my mind. What if Bradley had gone into the hollow to set some traps and Maggie had followed him to try to reason with him? What if they'd argued and he'd fallen? I hated to admit it, but that scenario made perfect sense.

"Penny for your thoughts?" Cody asked. We were sitting on the sofa looking into the flames of the fire as they randomly danced to their own tune.

I told him what I'd been thinking. I trusted Cody with my thoughts. In many ways I trusted him more than I trusted anyone else.

"I agree your logic makes sense," Cody replied as he slowly dragged a finger up and down my bare arm. His arm was around my shoulder and my head was on his chest and I felt myself relax for the first time in hours. "But that still doesn't explain either Grover's death or the presence of the black poker chip in either man's possession."

"You're right." I sat up straight. "The black chip in both men's pockets links them, and while Maggie might have argued with Bradley, resulting in an accident, she wouldn't have forced Grover into a boat and then forced him overboard." I let out a long sigh of relief. "She didn't do it."

"You really thought she had?"

"I thought she might have," I admitted. "Maggie is feisty. If the cats were in danger she'd take action. I'm not saying she'd kill anyone in cold blood, but she very well might have followed Bradley into the hollow and tried to talk some sense into him."

Suddenly my relief turned to terror. "If she didn't kill Bradley where is she?"

Cody hugged me to his body in a show of comfort. "I wish I knew."

We sat quietly for a few moments, each lost in our own thoughts.

"Did Maggie have her phone with her?" Cody asked.

"No. She said phones weren't allowed on the retreat."

"Do you have any idea where else she might have gone?" Cody asked. "Does she have a favorite spot where she likes to go to unwind and escape?"

"Not that I can think of. Besides, why would she lie about the yoga retreat? If she wanted a week away all she needed to do was say she wanted a week away. Why lie?"

Cody didn't answer right away.

"Is there anyone who might know where she actually went? Marley?"

Marley was Maggie's best friend and business partner. If Maggie was going to tell anyone the truth it would be her. "I'll call her to ask."

"It's late," Cody reminded me.

"I have to know."

"Just be careful what you tell her. We wouldn't want to worry her needlessly."

Cody was right. If I called Marley and asked her where Maggie really was and my aunt had lied to Marley as well as us, she'd be worried.

"I'll make something up about needing to get hold of her because Siobhan is on the island. I'll ask her if she has the contact info for the retreat. If Maggie told Marley she was actually doing something else I think she'll tell me. If she gives me the information for the retreat I'll know she lied to Marley too."

I called Marley, who quickly provided the information for the retreat. It was clear Maggie had lied to her best friend as well as her niece. Where could she be?

"I've been thinking about the man Danny mentioned," Cody said when I got off the phone with Marley. "The name Jeremy Vance sounds familiar. I seem to remember there being a piece about him in one of the articles I bought to fill out my first few editions of the paper. I'm going to head over to the newspaper to look through the archives."

I knew that while Cody tried to focus on local news, from time to time he purchased articles from the Associated Press for the empty spots when he couldn't get his advertising space filled up.

"I'll go with you," I offered.

Cody held my hand as we walked out to the car. Max and Ichabod both followed us and hopped into the backseat when Cody opened the door.

"It seems like Finn and Siobhan are getting along pretty well," he said as we drove toward Pelican Bay.

"Yeah. Seems like. I just hope she doesn't break his heart again."

"You think she will?" Cody asked.

"I think she might. Siobhan is my sister and I love her very much, but she tends to fritter from one person to the next. She has a short attention span when it comes to relationships and Finn is a forever kind of guy."

"I guess I can see how she might not be the settling-down sort. Still, I did catch her looking at him the entire time we were talking. If she stays long enough they might find a way to work things out and meet in the middle."

"I hope so. I care a lot about Finn."

Outside the paper, I grabbed Ichabod so he couldn't jump out and scurry away, and Cody escorted Max into the interior of the small office. I set the cat down once we were inside and he trotted back toward the morgue as if he knew where we were going. Cody opened the door and Ichabod trotted inside. He circled the room and then jumped up onto a shelf.

"Let's start there," I suggested.

"Those are the editions printed the first week I reopened the paper."

Cody and I each took one of the newspapers and began looking through it.

"Look at this." I pushed the paper toward Cody. There was a small article he had picked up as filler from a Canadian newspaper on the bottom of page eight.

"I remember that," Cody commented. "They found the body of a man on one of the islands in the

Georgia Strait. The man's boat had most likely gone down during that big storm that swept through the area a week or so before he was found. The man died of dehydration rather than drowning, so it was determined that he must have somehow made it to the island before he died. His name was Jeremy Vance."

"So that's why he stopped showing up at the Fisherman's Lodge," I concluded.

"Yeah, but what's even odder is that when they found his body there was a black poker chip in his pocket."

Chapter 9

Sunday, October 24

It had been two days since I'd discovered that Maggie hadn't attended the yoga retreat and yet there'd still been no word from her. I was beyond worried. Her original plan was to come home on Sunday evening, and I found myself clinging to the hope that she'd show up as planned and everything would be okay. Cody suggested that I let him handle the choir this week, but I needed something to keep my mind off the horrific scenarios stomping around my mind, demanding to be heard. I decided to do the only thing I could under the circumstances, which was to go about my day the best I could and hope that everything turned out okay.

We agreed not to mention to anyone that we didn't know where Maggie was until she failed to show up and we knew for certain she was missing. Why worry my mom and Marley and most of the other residents on the island unless we needed to? Cody, Finn, Danny, Siobhan, Tara, and I had spent the entire day Saturday trying to figure out where Maggie might have gone, but every lead we'd followed had ended up nowhere. There were only eight more hours until the last ferry of the day arrived. Only eight more hours left to wonder.

"Veronica says her throat hurts and she can't do her solo," Trinity Paulson informed me.

"She seemed fine just a while ago," I said.

Trinity shrugged. "That's just what she told me."

I looked around the room. I didn't see Veronica anywhere.

"Do you know where she went?" I asked.

"She left."

Terrific.

"Did you happen to notice if her parents came to get her?" The last thing I needed was a runaway ten-year-old who had been entrusted to my care.

"No, I didn't see her parents." Trinity hesitated. "I don't think her throat really hurt."

"No? So what do you think was wrong with her?"

Trinity nodded across the room to where Annabelle Sawyer was talking to some other girls.

Annabelle had truly been blessed with a magnificent voice. She could sing like an angel, but she was severely lacking in the personality department. Annabelle knew her voice was exceptional and fully expected to have every solo assigned to her without question. When Cody and I decided to occasionally spread the opportunity around, Annabelle could be venomous. If I had to guess she'd probably teased Veronica about being off key and the poor girl had scurried away with her tail between her legs.

"Thanks. I'll handle it," I told Trinity.

"Cait…"

"Yes?"

"If Destiny gives her baby to another family will I still be an aunt?"

I decided on a simple answer to a complicated question, given the fact that I really did need to track down Veronica. "You will most definitely still be an aunt, but if she gives the baby to another family you will be a different kind of aunt than your own Auntie Genevieve is to you."

"What do you mean?"

I placed my hand on Trinity's arm and gave it a slight squeeze. "I really need to go find Veronica. Maybe this is a conversation you should have with your mom."

"She never wants to talk about Destiny's baby. Mom is sad about it, but I want to be an aunt."

"Okay, then, how about if we talk about it later?" I imagined the prospect of being an aunt must be pretty exciting when you're eight.

"Okay."

I told Cody what I suspected had occurred between Veronica and Annabelle before I headed out to look for Veronica. He agreed to have a chat with Annabelle in my absence. Hopefully, we'd be able to get the issue resolved before the choir was scheduled to go on in less than fifteen minutes.

When I'd first been approached about working with the children's choir I'd been hesitant. I certainly didn't have any children of my own and wasn't sure I'd be any good at working with them. My mom had talked me into giving it a try, and I'm glad she did. I found I really enjoyed it, adolescent drama and all.

I found Veronica sitting near Father Kilian's koi pond. She looked so lost and alone.

"Trinity tells me you can't do your solo."

"My throat hurts."

"It was fine a little while ago when we were practicing," I reminded her.

Veronica didn't respond.

"Did Annabelle say something to you?"

Veronica sighed. "She said I had a dumb voice and I sounded like a cat in the blender when I tried to hit the high notes."

I took Veronica's hand. "Don't listen to Annabelle. You have a beautiful voice."

"Not as beautiful as hers."

"That's true."

Veronica looked surprised by my honesty.

"But just because you can't hit the high notes quite as well as she can doesn't mean you shouldn't sing. You'll do a lot of things in your life. Some of them you'll be the best at; others someone else will do better. But just because you aren't the best at something doesn't mean you shouldn't do it."

"No one wants to hear me sing." Veronica sighed. "Everyone wants to hear Annabelle."

"*I* want to hear you sing," I informed her. "Your parents want to hear you sing. And I know Cody wants to hear you sing. It was his idea to give you this solo in the first place. He said you'd be just right for it."

Veronica smiled. "He did?"

"He absolutely did. So will you do it?"

"Okay." Veronica hugged me around the neck.

We'd both stood up to return to the church when Veronica bent over and picked up something from the dirt surrounding the pond.

"Someone dropped this." She handed me a black poker chip.

My heart pounded in my chest as I considered the ramifications. "Why don't you go on inside and tell Cody you're going to sing? I'll be right in."

"Okay."

I looked around the area and didn't see any sign of a body to go with the chip, but the koi pond was covered in lily pads, so I wasn't able to see down to the bottom. My heart was pounding as I took out my phone and called Finn. I'd seen him arrive for Mass earlier, so I knew he was in the church. Cell phones weren't usually allowed inside, but Finn was given a pass due to the emergency status of a lot of his calls as long as he kept the ringer on vibrate.

Please, God, don't let there be a body to go with this chip.

Luckily, Finn didn't find a body in either the pond or on the surrounding grounds. The chip had been lying near the pond, so it made sense that someone must have dropped it. It didn't look as if it had been placed intentionally, so my money was on it having fallen from someone's pocket. Did the killer attend St. Patrick's? The thought was a lot more disturbing than I was prepared to deal with.

"Are you okay?" Cody asked me after services. He'd been inside directing the kids and so wasn't aware of what had happened until Mass was over.

"Yeah, I'm okay. I was totally freaked out at first, but Finn has done a pretty thorough search of the grounds and there hasn't been a body found. I was thinking I might talk to Father Kilian. I found the chip near the pond he tends every day. Maybe he saw someone lurking about."

"Father Kilian just got back from the retreat he was attending this week. In fact, we had to start Mass five minutes late because the ferry was a little behind schedule. I doubt he knows anything."

"That's right; I forgot he'd been away. Maybe I'll have a chat with Sister Mary instead."

"You can talk to her later. The softball game is about to start, and then we're all invited to your mom's for dinner. I'm pretty sure I overheard your mom invite both Father Kilian and Sister Mary."

"Okay. It can wait." I took Cody's hand in mine as we headed toward the ball field. As much as I tended to stress out about the fact that Sunday dinners at Mom's could become the staging area for soap-opera-strength drama, I was really looking forward to it today. For the first time in a very long time, all five Hart siblings would share a meal in the home of their birth. When I was growing up there was a standing tradition that every Hart on the island would gather at our house on Sunday. Back then, before Dad died and the cannery closed, there were dozens of Hart aunts, uncles, and cousins. Other than my own family and Aunt Maggie, all of the Hart relatives had moved away. There were times when dinner was attended by only myself, Cassie, and my mom. But it sounded like we would have a full house this week. I only wished Aunt Maggie could be here to round out the family.

"Caitlin, can you help Siobhan get the folding chairs from the attic?" my mom asked as soon as we arrived at her house after the game. "Bring them all down; we've got a full house today."

Full house was right. There had to be at least thirty people there. Not that I was complaining. I liked the energy a crowd provided.

"It's a good thing Mom made spaghetti," I commented. "It's easy to expand."

"I overheard her send Aiden to the market for additional bread and salad fixings, but it seems like she had plenty of sauce and pasta on hand," Siobhan said as we climbed the stairs.

"I really miss these big dinners," I added as we started up the final flight of stairs leading to the attic. "It just hasn't been the same since everyone moved away."

"I don't know that I miss the crowd, but I did miss Mom's cooking," Siobhan answered. "Takeout is fine; it gets you fed. But there's nothing like Mom's pasta."

"Or her stew."

"Or her homemade soups." Siobhan placed her hand on her stomach and rubbed it in a circular motion.

I opened the door to the attic and turned on the light. The room was packed with mementos of four generations of Harts. Maybe more, if you counted any items the family may have brought with them from Ireland.

"Do you see the chairs?" Siobhan asked.

"I think they're against the back wall."

It had been a while since we'd needed to use the chairs and quite a few boxes had been stacked in front of them. It was going to take a bit of elbow grease to retrieve them.

"Maybe we should have grabbed a couple of the guys," I realized.

"They were all watching the game. I don't think Mom wanted to disturb them. Does Finn always come to dinner on Sundays?"

"Not always. But he does come sometimes."

"I just figured once I moved away he'd stop coming."

"He's Danny's best friend. In a lot of ways he's part of the family," I pointed out.

"Yeah, I guess."

Siobhan began setting boxes to the side.

"So how is it?" I asked. "Seeing him again after all this time?"

Siobhan stopped what she was doing. She seemed to be considering my question.

"It's odd," she finally answered. "On one hand, it seems like a lifetime ago that we were a couple, yet the more time I spend with him, the more I realize how really normal and natural it feels. I'm not sure we'll ever be a couple again, but I do think we can and will be friends. I don't know why I thought friendship couldn't be an option for us."

"It probably wasn't an option in the beginning," I commented. "I mean, you did practically leave him at the altar."

"It wasn't at the altar. But yeah, I get what you're saying. I'm sure I hurt him deeply, and I'm sorry, but he seems to be willing to forgive me, so I guess we'll just build a new relationship on that. Is that my wedding dress?"

I looked into a closet at the far end of the room that had been left open. Hanging inside was both Mom's dress as well as the one Siobhan never had the chance to wear.

"Yeah. I don't know how the door got open."

"Now that I'm on the island and Finn and I are talking again, Mom is probably planning to pick up right where she left off."

"You think she thinks the wedding is back on?" I asked.

"I think she *hopes* the wedding is back on. She most likely had the dress out to check for size. I guess I need to have a talk with her." Siobhan sighed.

"Let me talk to her," I offered. "If you talk to her, you'll most likely end up in an argument. Maybe I can help her see that she's getting ahead of herself, if she indeed is seeing wedding bells in your not-so-distant future."

"Thanks, Cait. You're a good sister."

I smiled. Siobhan had said that to me twice since she'd been back. I'm sure she had no idea how much her words meant, but they sounded wonderful to me.

"That was fun," Cody said as we drove to the dock. I'd decided to meet the ferry to see for myself whether Aunt Maggie had returned as planned. Waiting to hear from her was literally killing me. "I have to admit that Sunday dinners at the Hart house are some of my fondest childhood memories. My family never did stuff together when I was a kid. I mean, we loved one another, but my parents had their own things and we kids had our own things. Other than holidays or special occasions we rarely even shared a meal together."

"Not even dinner?"

"Not usually. When I was really young my mom would feed us kids early and then she'd eat with my dad when he got home from work. When we got older we'd usually grab a sandwich and then eat in our rooms or head out to a friend's. I seem to remember Danny wasn't any happier than Cassie seems to be now about the forced family time, but I would have given quite a lot for a big, noisy family like yours."

"I guess you never really want what you have," I mused.

I tensed as we approached the ferry dock. I could see the boat in the distance. I didn't know what I was going to do if Maggie didn't drive off the car deck with the other travelers.

Cody parked near Coffee Cat Books. He took my hand as we walked to the disembarking area. I could feel my stomach begin to churn as the boat approached the dock. It took a few minutes for the crew to tie up before the passengers began to file off. I held my breath as first one car and then the next began to drive off.

"I don't see her," I said with a tone of panic in my voice.

"They still need to clear the lower level." Cody squeezed my hand.

"Maggie hates the lower level. She says it's too tight to park comfortably. She always arranges to park on the main level."

"Maybe she was late and didn't have a choice," Cody suggested.

I watched as red cars and blue cars and vans and trucks all filed from the vessel, but no Maggie. When the crew gave the all-clear signal I began to cry.

Chapter 10

The drive back to the peninsula seemed to take forever, but it actually took just a few minutes. I was never so happy in my life to see Maggie's car in the drive and the lights on inside her kitchen. I hopped out of the car and ran inside, where Maggie was having a cup of tea and chatting with her cat, Akasha.

"Oh my God, where have you been?" I threw myself into Maggie's arms and continued to sob.

"What's wrong?" Maggie hugged me tightly. "I told you I'd be away until today."

"But you weren't at the yoga retreat and then there were the murders.… I was so scared."

Maggie took a step back and looked me in the face. "What murders?"

Cody and I spent the next half hour catching Maggie up on everything that had been going on since she'd been gone, including the fact that Siobhan was currently staying with her.

"I can't believe Grover and the mayor are dead." Maggie looked as if she were in shock. "Who would do such a thing?"

"That's what we're trying to find out. We have a lot of theories, but none of them have panned out so far. Given the fact that both Bradley and Grover were members of the Island Council, we think their deaths might be related to something the council has going on."

"No wonder you were worried. I'm so sorry you had to go through that."

"Where were you?" I asked.

"I just needed to have some time to myself."

I wanted to push it, but I could see I wasn't going to get any more out of her. At least not for now. I looked out the window at the darkening sky. "I really should go to let Max out. The others are coming over to strategize. Why don't you join us? You knew the men as well as any of us. Maybe you can help."

"I'd be happy to come by. Just let me grab a sweater."

"Oh…" I turned just as I was about to go out Maggie's back door toward my cabin. "Siobhan borrowed your whiteboard so we could create a murder board. I hope you don't mind."

Maggie laughed. "I don't mind at all. Do you?"

"Why would I mind? It's not my board."

"That's not what I meant. Siobhan has a way of taking charge even when the thing she's taking over isn't really hers to control."

"I don't mind," I confirmed. "I'm just happy to have her home."

When Danny, Tara, Finn, and Siobhan arrived everyone greeted Maggie and then we set to work to try to figure out our next move. It seemed our little Scooby gang was growing. With the addition of Maggie this evening there were seven of us, plus Max and Ichabod.

Siobhan once again began the discussion. "I guess we should start by following up on the cats," she suggested. She looked at Maggie. "Francine informed us that Mayor Bradley was planning to have the cats removed from the hollow. Can you elaborate?"

Maggie glanced at me with a guilty look on her face. "I'm sorry I didn't tell you. I didn't want to worry you, and I was determined that I was going to stop him, one way or another."

"That's okay," I said, but I was certain my expression said anything but.

"I really am sorry."

"I'm not a baby anymore. You don't have to protect me."

"I know. Again, I'm sorry."

"So about the cats…" Siobhan brought us back on topic. "Why did Bradley want the cats gone anyway? I get that he isn't a fan of the species, but the cats in the hollow tend to stay there. They don't bother anyone."

"I really don't know why he was so adamant that the cats had to go," Maggie said. "And I find it more than a little disturbing that he died in the hollow. What was he doing there in the first place?"

"We don't know," I admitted.

"Are we thinking that someone killed Bradley over the issue of the cats?" Maggie asked.

"Honestly, I kind of doubt it," I answered. "For one thing, we have two council members dead, and I can't see how Grover ties in with the cats. For another, I can't think of anyone who would actually commit murder over the cat issue except for you and me, and I'm pretty sure we didn't do it. At least *I* didn't do it."

I looked pointedly at Maggie.

"*I* didn't do it," Maggie defended herself.

"Okay, then, if the mall isn't the motive and the cats aren't either, what is?" Siobhan asked. "Are there any other hot-button issues the council is working on?" She looked at Maggie.

Maggie sat quietly. I imagined she was considering Siobhan's question. Although the reason we were all gathered was unsettling, it was nice to have everyone working together.

"There's one thing, but I have a hard time believing anyone would kill two men over it," Maggie began. "Shortly after Francine and I were elected to the council, Bradley suggested we might want to take a look at some of the companies the island contracts with for certain services."

"Like what?" I asked.

"Like garbage removal and street maintenance. These services are provided by private companies based in larger cities such as Seattle. The parent companies hold the contracts with the council and they staff a local office to actually provide the services. Bradley seemed to be pushing for the council to put the services out to bid. I'm not sure why it came up at this point, but the rest of the council were of the opinion that the companies we currently contract with were doing a good job. No one really wanted to mess with a competitive-bidding process."

"Yeah, why fix what isn't broken?" Tara commented.

"Why would Bradley even want to mess with such an expensive and time-consuming process if the council is happy with the contractors they're currently working with?" Siobhan asked.

"Kickbacks," Danny guessed.

"After considering the issue I believe Danny is probably right," Maggie confirmed. "Although I should state that I have no proof of it one way or the other."

"So someone was bribing him to turn the contracts over to them," I clarified.

"Yes. The issue seemed to heat up about six weeks ago, when out of the blue Bradley managed to get Grover to go along with his idea. Byron was on the fence, but I could see he was waffling under pressure from Bradley and Grover."

"So who would have motive to kill them?" Tara asked.

"The men who currently hold the contracts," Maggie answered. "The refuse contract alone is worth millions of dollars a year. If the service went out to bid chances are a new company hoping to get a foothold in the area would underbid the current contractor to force a change."

"Can you get us a list of all the companies that would be affected, as well as the names of the owners of those companies?" Cody asked.

"I can. If I had to guess I'd say the person with the most to lose should the council vote to put the contacts out to bid would be Dougan Flounder. He's the only contractor who's based locally."

"And what does he do?" Siobhan asked.

"He takes care of the landscaping and maintenance of all the public areas such as parks and walkways. He has a year-round staff that's been with him for a number of years, and I know he pays them well. I won't say he's expensive exactly, but I do think he would lose in a bidding war to a larger corporation should it come down to that."

"I'll talk to him tomorrow," I offered. "He comes into the bookstore for coffee most mornings, so maybe I can catch him then, although I'd say the guy doesn't seem like he has a violent bone in his body."

"I have to agree with that," Maggie offered her opinion.

Siobhan turned and looked at the board. She held the marker to her chin as she appeared to study what we had. I sat back and tried to make sense of it all. The issue with the cats provided an emotional motive, whereas the one with the contracts provided a financial one. I couldn't help thinking of the saying about love and money.

Ichabod jumped into my lap and began swatting me in the face. I hadn't paid as much attention to him as I probably should have since he'd been with me. I was admittedly busy, but that really wasn't an excuse. I knew my time with the cats that came into my life was short, so I usually tried to make the most of what we had.

"I'm going to check Ichabod's food and water," I announced. "I'll be right back."

I headed toward the kitchen, but the cat headed up the stairs. Maybe it was the cat box that needed attention. I followed my feline friend up to the loft and headed to the cat box. Ichabod jumped up onto the dresser and began swatting things onto the floor. I was about to tell him to knock it off when I remembered previous feline visitors and their fortuitous rearrangement of my personal possessions.

I looked closely at each item as I picked it up. I doubted my hairbrush held a clue, or the new earrings I'd recently purchased at the farmers market either. There was a flyer for the Halloween party the town was holding on Main Street next weekend. The event was usually a lot of fun. Maybe I'd ask Cody if he wanted to go with me. I put the flyer in my pocket so I'd remember to ask him and then picked up the only other item on the floor: my car keys. Cody had picked me up that morning, so I hadn't needed to take the keys with me. I picked them up off the floor and looked at them.

Then I looked at Ichabod. "These are my car keys."

He meowed and rubbed against my leg.

I remembered that I'd found it odd that Bradley's car hadn't been found at the entrance to the hollow, from which one was required to continue on foot. Grover had floated in from a boat, we'd assumed, so his vehicle hadn't been on-site either. I wondered if Finn had managed to track down either car yet.

After I checked Ichabod's cat box for good measure, I headed back down the stairs. The group had taken a break and Tara was serving them beverages and cake left over from my mother's dinner.

"Did you track down either Bradley's or Grover's car?" I asked Finn.

"No. Neither vehicle was at the victim's home. Grover's wasn't parked at any of the marinas on the island and Bradley's wasn't on or near any of the access roads to the hollow. I've told everyone who works law enforcement on the island to keep an eye out for both vehicles. It's a small island, so I'm sure they'll turn up eventually."

I thought about the keys. I had the feeling Ichabod wanted me to do something more proactive than just wait for someone to stumble across the vehicles.

"Yes, the island is small, but that doesn't necessarily mean the vehicles will be found," I countered. "They could be inside a shed or a garage, or camouflaged in some way. I think we need to actively look for them. I wonder if either vehicle had a GPS system. Both sedans were fairly new."

"I'll check." Finn excused himself to make a phone call.

"Okay, where were we?" Siobhan asked after everyone except Finn returned to the living room.

"While my gut tells me that the motive behind the murders is one that would apply to both men, I can't help but remember when I believed Maggie's poisoning and Keith Weaver's death were related," I began. "I was wrong about that and we could be wrong about this as well. There's speculation that Bradley was having an affair. While I'm not sure that's a strong motive, it still might be interesting to find out who Bradley was sleeping with. I'm willing to bet someone saw them together." I looked at Maggie. "The Bait and Stitch is gossip central on the island. Ask around. See who knows what."

"Aye, aye, Captain." Maggie saluted me while Siobhan wrote our aunt's assignment down on the murder board.

Finn came back into the room. "I have a hit on Grover's car. I'm heading out to check it out right now."

Siobhan handed me the dry erase marker. "I'll go with you."

Now there were five.

"I've had a long couple of days," Maggie announced. "If you're done with me I think I'll head back to the house."

I wanted to demand that she tell me where she'd been all week, but I supposed it was none of my business, so I just kissed her on the cheek and told her that I'd catch up with her the next day.

"I really should go as well," Tara announced. "I hate to leave Destiny alone."

"I thought you were staying at Maggie's."

"We were, but now that Maggie's back it seems silly. I doubt we're dealing with some random serial killer. I think Destiny and I will be fine on our own." Tara looked at Danny. "I let Destiny use my car to take her sisters home after dinner at your mom's. Can I catch a ride with you?"

"Absolutely."

And now there were two.

I looked at Cody. "Do you need to go as well?"

"Do you want me to?"

"No."

"I can stay. Do you want to go over the murder board some more?"

"No."

"Are you thinking of picking up where we left off in my office?"

"Yes, please."

Chapter 11

Tuesday, October 26

I focused on the steady rhythm of my feet hitting the hard-packed sand as I followed Max down the beach. Today the community would lay Grover Cloverdale to rest. Although the circumstances surrounding his death hinted at situations that hadn't yet been made public, Grover had been a popular man on the island who'd had many friends and admirers. It was a beautiful sunny day, and it seemed likely most of the island's residents would come out to bid a last farewell to the man who had been a good neighbor for so very many years.

I really should be at the cabin primping for the midmorning event, but the past few days had proven to be an emotional roller coaster that had spun my head more than I'd care to admit. Both Mayor Bradley's and Grover Coverdale's cars had been found by Finn on Sunday evening in the abandoned barn of a longtime island resident named Pritchett Farrell. Pritchett had been visiting family in New Jersey for most of the summer and so wasn't considered a suspect in the killing of either man. The fact that Pritchett lived off the beaten path led Finn to believe that whoever the killer was, he or she was familiar with the island and the goings and comings of its residents.

The idea that the killer was most certainly a local left me with a feeling of dread. I couldn't think of a single person I wouldn't be devastated to discover had carried out such a calculated and personal crime.

And then there was Maggie... I'd asked several times where she'd been during her week away, and for whatever reason, she absolutely refused to tell me. When I mentioned that no one from the ferry had seen her leave, she told me that her plans had changed and she had actually remained on the island. I asked her where on the island she'd gone and she'd very politely told me it was none of my business.

Maybe it wasn't, but I found I still really wanted to know.

Besides, if she had been on the island she couldn't have helped but have heard about the deaths of the two men; yet when I'd informed her of their demises upon her return, she'd seemed genuinely surprised.

The only conclusion I could come to was that she either was lying about staying on the island or she'd been holcd up in a location that had no access to the rest of the world. If that were the case, why would she do it?

I'd almost suspected Maggie'd had something to do with the men's deaths, but the truth of the matter was that she really had been trying to help. She'd managed to uncover the fact that while Nora Bradley fully intended to divorce her husband, Grover and his wife had been working on a reconciliation before he died. Maggie also found out that at least part of Bradley's financial crisis stemmed from the fact that his rich wife had cut him off, though it seemed the depth of his debt indicated the problem had been going on for a long time.

As for the rumors of the mayor's affair, it turned out that the identity of his mistress was the best-kept secret the island had ever known.

I paused when we came to the jetty. It would be best to turn around if I was going to catch a shower before Cody came by to pick me up. As for my relationship with him, it had caused as much emotional turmoil over the last couple of days as anything else, but in a good way. Cody and I hadn't actually... well, you know, but we were definitely heading in that direction. The only hesitation on either of our parts seemed to stem from our complicated past. I was pretty sure I was ready to move past that, and if past events were any indication, Cody was ready to move on as well.

Back home, I dried and fed Max and then headed upstairs to the shower. My funeral dress was getting a lot more use than I would have liked. We'd laid Mayor Bradley to rest the previous day and it hadn't been that long ago that several other island favorites had suffered unnatural deaths. There were times I wondered what the world was coming to, but the truth of the matter was, murder among neighbors wasn't a new concept; it had just taken a bit longer to take a foothold on the island I call home.

Ichabod was sitting in the window of my loft bedroom looking out at the sea. I wondered if he was planning his next move or if he was simply watching the pair of bald eagles that were circling in the sky, looking for their breakfast. I would be sorry to see Ichabod go when he left. He was an easygoing cat, though a bit pushy at times. At any rate, he seemed to fit in well with Max and me.

"I'm going to be away a good part of the day," I explained to both of the animals. "I've refilled your food and water dishes and I'll be home as soon as I'm able."

Max barked. I doubted he knew what I was saying, but I had no doubt Ichabod understood perfectly.

It was nice to have a sunny day for the service. It seemed the majority of the funerals I'd been to as of late had taken place under cloudy skies.

"It's downright depressing to attend two funerals in two days," Doris Rutherford, the queen bee of the island's gossip hotline, commented as we waited for the graveside service to begin.

I looked to the front of the crowd, where Grover's wife was being comforted by their eldest son. I felt so very bad for them. I couldn't imagine losing someone I loved in such an unexpected manner.

"It has been a difficult couple of weeks," I agreed.

"I certainly hope Finn figures out who did this soon," she continued. "It's disconcerting to realize we may be living on an island with a cold-blooded killer."

"I'm sure Finn is doing everything he can."

"You would think that with two deaths in such a short period of time the FBI would be called in," Doris added.

"I think the FBI only investigates federal and bistate crimes. This is neither. Would you excuse me for a minute? I need to go give Siobhan a message."

Doris looked toward the front of the crowd, where my sister was surrounded by pretty much everyone. There was no doubt about it; now that the islanders knew Siobhan was home she'd stepped right back into her role as the social center. There are some people who demand attention by their very presence and Siobhan was one of them.

I didn't really need to talk to her; I'd just wanted to get away from Doris, so I headed toward the far edge of the cemetery, where Tara was waiting with Destiny for the service to begin. Both Danny and

Cody had been enlisted to serve as pallbearers, so they were occupied for the time being.

"Big crowd," I stated the obvious. "Even larger than Bradley's funeral yesterday."

"Bradley might have been the mayor, but he had questionable morals and a lot of folks didn't really like him," Tara pointed out. "I've been hearing rumors that if he had lived he probably wouldn't have been reelected next time around. Grover, on the other hand, was generally well-liked. He was a bit more pro-development than I preferred, but he seemed to be honest and aboveboard."

"I wonder who they're going to get to be mayor now," I said.

"Good question. There are three remaining council members, but I don't see any of them wanting to do it. It's really a full-time job and Maggie is pretty busy with the Bait and Stitch, while both Francine and Byron seem happy in retirement. What we need is some young blood on the council. Someone like you."

"Thank you, but no, thank you. I'm not cut out for politics. Besides, I'm pretty busy myself. I'd suggest Cody, but he has his hands full getting the paper up and running."

"What about Aiden?" Destiny asked.

"He'd be a great mayor, but I don't see him giving up fishing to do it. We really need a mayor who's around all year, not for just part of it."

"I'm sure the council will find someone," Tara assured me.

"It looks like they're going to start," I told them.

"Mrs. Cloverdale looks so sad," Destiny whispered.

"Yeah," I agreed. "She really does."

The service was lovely, and when all was said and done, there wasn't a dry face in the crowd. The Cloverdales were holding a reception in the community center, so everyone headed in that direction once Grover had been laid to rest.

"Caitlin, dear, I'm so glad I ran into you," said Velmalee Arlington, the head of the community theater group, soon after we arrived.

"How are you, Velmalee?" I asked as I picked up a piece of cheese from the tray that was being circulated.

"I'm fine, thank you. I was wondering if you would be willing to help me with the haunted house at the school fund-raiser on Thursday. I've had several volunteers call and cancel on me at the last minute."

I was about to refuse because I was already so busy with the murder investigation and everything else I had going on in my life, but then I saw the look of desperation in the woman's eyes. Velmalee was flamboyant by any standards, but she was a nice woman and I knew the haunted house was a fund-raiser for the sixth-grade trip.

"What time do you need me?" I asked.

"Around three would be perfect."

"And how long will you need me?"

"We should be done by seven."

"Okay," I agreed. "I'll need to check with Tara because that will mean my leaving the bookstore early, but as long as she doesn't need me I'll be there."

Velmalee smiled. "Wonderful. And it would be perfect if you would dress as a zombie."

"A zombie?"

"Yes. I'll see you then."

I waved as Velmalee walked away. When she'd asked me to help, I'd thought she wanted me to do something boring like sell tickets or run the snack bar. But playing the part of a zombie would be fun. Maybe I'd see if Cody wanted to be a zombie with me. I was sure Velmalee would welcome the extra help and going as a zombie couple sounded like a good datelike activity.

"What are you smiling about?" Tara asked as she approached me from across the room.

"I'm going to be a zombie."

"Sounds like fun."

"I think it will be, but I'll need to get off early on Thursday. Velmalee wants me at the haunted house by three."

"I think Destiny and I can cover things."

"I figured you wouldn't mind, but I told Velmalee that I'd need to check with you before I could commit."

"I appreciate that." Tara looked around the room. "Have you seen Danny?"

I scanned the place. "No. Do you need him for something?"

"No," Tara admitted. "I was just curious whether he was still here or if he'd left."

"I haven't seen him since we first arrived. Danny isn't one to enjoy this type of thing, so I wouldn't be surprised if he left."

Tara pursed her lips. "I figured."

It sounded like Tara was more than just a little annoyed that Danny hadn't stayed.

"Is something wrong?" I asked.

"No, nothing's wrong. I think I'll see if they need help in the kitchen."

Something was wrong. I'd known Tara my whole life and I was well acquainted with her nothing's-wrong voice. I didn't want to get in the middle of whatever Tara and Danny were currently engaged in, so I started across the room in the opposite direction. I hadn't gotten very far when Siobhan stopped me.

"I have some new dirt on Bradley," Siobhan whispered in my ear. "I think we should meet tonight and update the murder board."

"You're really digging this, aren't you?"

Siobhan smiled. "I really am. Not only does it give me something to do other than spend all day contemplating my pathetic life but it gives me an excuse to spend time with Finn."

"So things are good between you?"

She looked around the room. No one was paying a bit of attention to us, but Siobhan suddenly seemed nervous. "Yeah, things are good. I mean, we aren't together or anything, but we're getting along and having fun. It's almost like old times. I hadn't realized how much I missed him. How much I missed all of this."

"So you might stay?"

Siobhan frowned. "I don't know. I really don't have any reason to go back to Seattle, but I have no idea what I could do to earn a living on the island. There aren't a lot of openings for executive assistants with a background in marketing and event planning. Maybe I can open my own business. Do you think the island needs an events planner?"

"I don't think there are a lot of people here who spend a lot of money throwing elaborate parties the way they do in the city. Maybe you could do weddings?"

"Now that would be ironic. I fled the island initially because planning my own wedding had become too overwhelming and here I am talking about coming back to the island as a wedding planner."

"You didn't leave because of the wedding planning," I put forth. "You were always superorganized and a wiz at planning even the most complex event."

"Yeah, I guess you're right. Still, I really don't know what I'm going to do. I guess I should give it some serious thought. It's not like I can stay with Maggie forever."

"I'm sure she's thrilled to have you. She has a full life, but I think she gets lonely rambling around that big house by herself. When I first moved into the cabin I went up to the house all the time, but now with the store and my other commitments I don't hang out with Maggie as much as I once did."

"Siobhan!" One of her old friends walked up. "You must come and meet my husband. We met in Paris when I did my tour after college."

Siobhan hugged her friend. "I'd love to meet your guy." She turned to me. "Tonight?"

"Tonight."

Chapter 12

Cody had offered to bring everyone dinner from Antonio's, which we completely devoured before we began our discussion. Siobhan was disappointed when Finn called to cancel, blaming it on a pile of paperwork that needed his attention. If I had to guess, he just wanted to slow things down a bit to avoid a repetition of the broken heart he'd never really gotten over.

"Now that we've all had a chance to eat let's start," Siobhan began. "I'll go first. I spoke to Mrs. Cloverdale at the reception today and she told me that her husband had had a falling out with Mayor Bradley over a business deal the two men had teamed up to invest in. She didn't know the specifics of the deal, but she did say that Grover had suffered quite a bit of angst over the whole thing, to the point where he had become almost impossible to live with. After Bradley was found dead, Grover went to his wife and asked her to forgive him for his moodiness. He assured her that he was going to fix whatever needed fixing so they could return to some semblance of normalcy. The next thing she knew, he was dead. She has no idea how he ended up in the water, but she seemed certain his death was the result of the deal he'd entered into with Bradley."

"And she just shared all this with you during her husband's funeral reception?" I asked.

Siobhan shrugged. "I have a way with people. They talk to me. So what do you think? Do we have our motive?"

"It would seem that we might," I agreed. "We know Bradley might have been having an affair, but I don't see how that would lead to Grover's death, and we know Bradley wanted the cats gone, but I don't see how that would affect Grover. The desire of the men to bid out the contracts currently held by the island seems to provide a motive, but Cody and I checked out all the companies involved, and while they would stand to lose a certain amount of revenue, with the exception of Dougan's firm, they're all large companies with multiple contracts. I'm guessing they deal with things like that all the time."

"So what about Dougan?" Tara asked.

"I had a fairly long conversation with him. He didn't seem overly worried about losing the business. He said he'd contracted with the island for quite a while and he'd always received positive reviews.

While the competitive bid could ruin what he'd built here, he had no reason to believe the council would actually follow through with Bradley's suggestion. He also said it was his understanding that it was really the refuse contract Bradley was after. If kickbacks were involved, there are quite a few huge conglomerates that would welcome a foothold on the islands and could afford to bribe someone to open the door for them."

"The refuse contract is a big one," Danny said. "If Bradley was after it, it wouldn't be too much of a stretch to think the current contractor might be feeling threatened. I get that the company is owned by a larger firm on the mainland, but the management and staff who operate on the island could lose their jobs if there was a change."

"That's true." I nodded. "I hadn't thought about that, but companies do tend to bring in their own staff when they move into an area. Especially their own management staff. I suppose the idea might deserve a second look."

"Okay," Siobhan said. "Cait and Cody will take another look at the competitive bid process as a motive, but in the meantime let's talk some more about the idea of a business deal gone bad. It seems like a likely motive that should be explored in more depth. The question is, how do we find out what they were up to?"

"I've been thinking about that," Danny answered. "I think we need to try to retrace the steps of both men the week before their deaths. Chances are one or both of them came into contact with the killer on more than one occasion."

"I agree." I stood up and walked over to the murder board. We had a lot of items that might have seemed relevant earlier but didn't seem to connect now that we were focused on the business angle.

"I think we need to re-sort these clues," I said. "We should keep only the ones that pertain to both men. Bradley's affair probably isn't relevant, nor is the fact that he was getting a divorce. The black poker chips are a linking clue, as is the fact that the cars were found in the same location."

"If the men were involved in a business deal, even a shady one, there must be a paper trail somewhere," Cody pointed out.

"Maybe I should call Lacy," Tara suggested. "She might know what sort of business deal Grover was in to."

"How would she know when his wife didn't?" Danny asked.

"I told you: she snoops."

"I guess it couldn't hurt to ask," I said.

I refilled everyone's beverages while Tara made her call. I felt like we had a lot of information that didn't quite fit together. I'd planned to suggest to Maggie that she not have Lacy over to clean again, but I did sort of hope she had something that would help us track down the killer.

"Lacy wasn't home, so I left a message," Tara informed us.

"I can stop by both men's offices tomorrow to see if I can pick up any clues," Cody offered. "Glenda seemed fine with me looking around Bradley's office the other day, and I think Wendy is still holding down the fort at Grover's place."

"Wait." I got up and crossed the room to pick up my backpack. "I totally forgot to drop off the document Wendy left on the copier last week."

I pulled out the sheet of paper and began to read. It was some kind of contract. Actually, it looked more like the draft of a contract rather than an actual contract itself.

"It looks like Bradley was planning to sell trees," I stated.

"Trees?" Tara asked. "What kind of trees?"

"It doesn't say, but based on the location indicated on the proposal it looks like they planned to harvest the trees from the hollow."

"Not the Madronas!" Tara groaned.

"That's why Bradley wanted to get rid of the cats," Danny said. "He couldn't very well orchestrate a large logging operation with all those cats there."

"That makes sense." Siobhan turned to write down the new information on the whiteboard.

"We know Nora Bradley owns the land where the hollow is located. Now it looks as if her husband planned to enter into a deal to sell the trees growing on that land. How does Grover fit into all of this?" Cody asked.

I frowned. How *did* Grover fit in?

"We know Bradley was having financial issues, so maybe Grover was providing the financial backing to get the project off the ground," Siobhan suggested.

"Maybe, but the rumor is that Grover was struggling financially as well," I reminded my sister.

Siobhan shrugged. "Then I have no idea."

"Of course you and me having money problems and old money having them aren't the same thing," I realized. "Grover had assets, even if he was short on cash. A lot of them. Real estate, cars, antiques. We know Nora controlled most of the money the Bradleys had, but Grover is the direct descendant of his family's wealth, so maybe he was going to finance the project. I think this bears further research."

Siobhan's cell phone dinged, indicating she had a text. She looked at it and frowned. "I have to make a call."

While Siobhan was out of the room the rest of us sat around and discussed the possible angles a little longer. Then Tara decided she needed to go home to see how Destiny was getting along and Danny went with her.

"Looks like it's just you and me." Cody pulled me into his arms.

"Looks like." I leaned forward and kissed him.

"I have something I want to talk to you about."

"You want to *talk*?"

"Actually, I want to kiss you again, but maybe we should talk first."

"Okay." I took a step back. Cody sounded so serious, which kind of frightened me. "What do you want to talk about?"

"Maybe we should take a walk."

"A walk?"

"Max looks like he might need to go out."

"Okay," I said, although I was thinking *what the heck?*

Cody held my hand as we started down the beach. It was a beautiful evening. The moon shone down on the calm water that lapped gently onto the shore. It was chilly, but Cody's body felt warm next to mine. I don't know why, but I was terrified this was the last romantic walk we would take together.

"You and I seem to be moving toward something," Cody began.

I held my breath as I waited for him to continue. *Please, God, don't say you want to cool things down just when they're heating up.*

"Due to our past experience, where a misunderstanding led to heartache," Cody continued, "I wanted to be sure that the *something* we're moving toward is the same in both our minds."

I frowned. "Okay. Why don't you tell me where you think we're headed and then I'll let you know if I think the same thing?"

Cody took a deep breath. He stopped walking and turned toward me. Then he took both my hands in his and looked me directly in the eye. "You know I'm attracted to you, and I think we both know we're heading toward a physical intimacy of the complete kind."

God, I hoped so.

"And I want so very badly to make love to you, but I need to be clear with you that what I'm after is something more."

"More?" I could feel my heart pounding as I waited for the other shoe to drop. I knew he was so going to tell me that we needed to take a step back from the intimacy we'd been building. He needed more than I could give him. I was after all only his best friend's kid sister.

"I love you. I've always loved you. I didn't admit it at the time, but the reason I came back to Madrona Island was to be with you. I'm not saying we need to run out and get married, but before we go any further I need you to understand that this isn't a fling for me. When I make love to you, I'll be making a forever kind of commitment. I know that once I share that with you there'll be no turning back."

I didn't say anything. I wanted to, but I was afraid I might cry.

"Cait?"

I let out the breath I'd been holding. "I love you too," I sobbed. Tears streamed down my face. The heck with holding them back.

"You do?"

"I do."

Cody pulled me into his arms and kissed me. A deep kiss filled with longing and meaning. I felt his heart meld with mine as the world faded away. The kiss seemed to last a lifetime, but before I knew it he was pulling back.

"Maybe we should go back to the cabin," he murmured.

"Oh, God, yes."

Chapter 13

Thursday, October 28

Cody and I shared a magical night we knew sealed a commitment for both of us. I asked him to spend the night, but he didn't want Mr. Parsons to worry, and honestly, I was just as happy to have some time to process everything that had happened. Cody was the man I'd always known I was meant to spend my life with, and for the first time I felt confident I was the woman for him as well.

In spite of the fact that I lay awake most of the night replaying Cody's gentle touch over and over in my mind, I woke up early the next morning and decided to take Max for a run before I headed into town. I dressed in layers and headed downstairs to see Siobhan sitting in my living room.

"What are you doing here so early?" I asked. My heart sank when I noticed the bags by her feet.

"I'm heading out on the first ferry east. My friend Rain is going to give me a ride into town so I don't have a lot of time, but I wanted to say good-bye before I left."

"You're leaving? Did something happen between you and Finn?"

"No. Things are fine between me and Finn. Or at least they were. I'm not so sure now. He seemed pretty upset when I called him earlier."

"I'll bet. It seemed like you might get back together."

"I guess we were headed in that direction, but my old boss called me last night. He offered me my job back. Actually, not the job I had before. He offered me a promotion and a huge raise. He said the company was lost without me."

"So you're going back? Just like that?"

Siobhan took a deep breath. It looked as if she were searching for the right words. "I've had so much fun being here on the island. I didn't realize how much I missed you and everyone else. I feel at home here in a way I've never felt in Seattle, but we've talked about the fact that there aren't any job opportunities here. I mean, really, what am I going to do? Get a waitressing job?"

Siobhan wasn't wrong about that.

"I'm so sorry I let us drift apart the way I did and I promise to visit more often, but I think I need to hear what my old boss has to say at the very least. I haven't committed to anything yet, and I plan to go into my meeting with him with an open mind, but the job I'm being offered is a dream come true."

"What about Finn?" I asked.

Siobhan looked up toward the sky the way I knew she did when she was fighting tears. "I love Finn. I've always loved Finn. But I would wither and die if I spent my days doing nothing more than changing diapers and going to PTA meetings. I need the challenge of a good negotiation or a problem to solve. I need to be able to use my planning and marketing skills. I need a life where I'm free to be the person I know I'm meant to be."

"Does Maggie know you're leaving?"

"Yeah, I told her. She's upset, but I think she understands. At least she said she did."

I crossed the room and hugged my big sister. I squeezed my arms as tightly around her as I could. She said she'd visit more often, but she wouldn't.

Siobhan took a step back and looked me in the eye. "You look different."

I blushed.

"You and Cody?"

"Me and Cody."

Siobhan hugged me again. "I'm so happy for you. I always felt there was something special between you. I really want to talk to you about this, but I have to go. If I miss the first ferry I'll be late for my meeting. I'll call you tonight."

"Okay." I felt like I was going to cry.

Siobhan hugged me again and then scurried out the door as Rain pulled up in the drive.

I watched the car move away and then headed upstairs to change into work clothes because I was no longer going to have time for a run with Max. I felt bad that he and I didn't have as much time to spend together as we once did. I know he likes hanging out with Cody, but I also know he misses me. I'm not sure how I'm going to reorganize my life so we can hang out more together, but I need to address the issue sooner rather than later.

I took a quick shower, then pulled on a pair of jeans and a Coffee Cat Books T-shirt. I headed downstairs and was preparing to leave when Ichabod began scratching at the door.

"I need to get to work. Can we do this later?"

Ichabod just looked at me.

"I promised Tara I'd be on time today."

"Meow." Ichabod began scratching again.

"Oh, okay. Let me call Tara to let her know I'm going to be late and then I'm all yours."

Tara said she was fine with me being late and then I went back to where Ichabod was waiting for me. I opened the door. "What do you want me to do?"

He trotted outside and headed toward my car.

"Oh, this should be interesting."

I opened the door for him and he jumped into the front seat. I noticed Max watching us through the window, so I went back for him and let him into the backseat.

I wasn't sure how I was supposed to take directions from a cat, but I have an open mind about these things and decided to just go with it. I figured Ichabod wanted to go somewhere farther than the peninsula because we most likely would have walked otherwise, so I headed down the road to the highway. "Okay, which way? Left or right?"

"Meow."

"Meow left or meow right?" I asked.

Ichabod just looked at me.

"How about this: one meow for left and two meows for right."

"Meow."

I followed Ichabod's meow instructions across the island to the north shore. Eventually, he directed me to a dirt road that led to a private drive. The house looked deserted and there was no sign of a car, but there was a boat tied to the dock that I recognized as belonging to one of the local fishermen.

"Are you sure?" I asked Ichabod.

"Meow."

"I'm not sure the person who lives here is going to be all that receptive to early morning visitors. Maybe we should come back later."

Ichabod began scratching at the passenger side window.

"Okay. Here goes nothing, but if we get yelled at don't say I didn't warn you."

I walked up to the front door with Max and Ichabod trailing behind me. I knocked twice, but no one answered. I was trying to decide what to do when Ichabod pushed the door open with his paw. Whoever had been the last one out hadn't closed it all the way.

"Hello," I called as I poked my head in the front door.

There was no answer, but there was a powerful smell that almost caused me to turn around, but Ichabod trotted on inside.

"Anyone here?" I called as I placed my hand over my nose and took a step inside the entry. "It's Caitlin Hart," I added as I walked down the dark, narrow hallway toward the back of the structure.

The first thing I noticed upon entering the living area was the pile of black poker chips on the dining room table. The next thing I saw was Leif Piney, lying dead on his living room floor.

"Poor Finn," Tara said later that morning after I filled her in on both the fact that we had a third victim and Siobhan had had a job offer. "I really thought Siobhan was enjoying being home."

"She was. But she needs to feel needed."

"She did an awesome job with the murder board."

"Yes, she did. And if we had a murder to solve every week we might be able to keep her interest. It's going to seem so odd to have her gone," I said. "I mean, I know she was only back for a little over a week, but I'd gotten used to having her around. It almost felt like old times, before Dad died and the cannery closed and everyone moved away."

Tara crossed the room and gave me one of her perfect Tara hugs. I hugged her back as I allowed my heart to long for a relationship with my sister that I knew I would never have.

"Am I interrupting something?" Destiny asked as she entered the main part of the store from the office.

"No, you aren't interrupting," I answered. "What do you need?"

"There's a call for Cait."

"Okay, thanks."

I headed into the office and picked up the receiver.

"This is Cait," I said.

A deep voice said, "If you value your life stay out of that which is none of your business."

The line went dead.

"That was weird."

"What's weird?" Tara asked as she came into the office.

I told her what the voice on the phone had said.

"Someone knows you're investigating. Maybe you should do as the caller said and leave the investigation to Finn."

"No way."

"The person on the phone threatened to kill you," Tara insisted.

"It wouldn't be the first time."

I couldn't help but notice the troubled look on Tara's face.

"Don't worry," I added. "I'll be careful. I'm going to be at the haunted house all afternoon. I doubt I'll be in any danger there."

"I don't know about that. You seem to have a knack for putting yourself in danger anywhere you go."

"I'll be careful," I repeated. "I promise."

Tara didn't say anything, but I could see she was worried.

"You don't think we have a serial killer on the island, do you?" Tara asked.

"I doubt it."

"We do have three bodies."

"Yeah, but my gut tells me they're connected, not random. A serial killer wouldn't know Bradley hated cats and Grover was afraid of water."

"How about Leif? Did his death indicate he died in a manner that addressed a fear or dislike?"

I frowned. "Actually, no. It appeared he was hit on the head with something, although I didn't really see anything I would consider to be a murder weapon. Of course it smelled pretty bad in the house, so I didn't stick around to look."

"The addition of Leif as a victim seems to change the focus of the investigation," Tara commented. "When the victims were just Bradley and Grover it seemed like the most obvious link was the council or the business deal, but Leif wasn't on the Island Council and he wasn't part of the tree harvesting deal. Assuming all three men were killed by the same person, I think we need to look for a new motive."

"They all belong to the Fisherman's Lodge. I suppose the killer could somehow be related to their activities there. The fact that both Grover and Bradley were found with black chips in their pockets and Leif had a whole pile of them on his dining room table seems to indicate that they're relevant."

"Maybe Leif killed Bradley and Grover for some reason and someone found out and killed him. Was there a chip on Leif's body?"

"Not that I noticed, but I didn't look through his pockets. I can ask Finn. If you ask me, though, I'd say Leif was the first victim rather than the last."

Tara scrunched up her nose. "Really? You think he's been dead for over a week?"

"Based on the condition of the body I'd say it's possible. I'm not a medical examiner, but I can tell you that man had been dead for quite some time. Finn will be able to answer that question for certain. I thought I might call him tonight to see how he's doing anyway."

Tara and I returned to the sales floor just as the noon ferry arrived. We'd found Thursdays weren't usually busy in the off season, but we didn't want to leave Destiny alone to deal with the few customers we'd undoubtedly have. I planned to check in with Amanda today to see how she was getting along with Angel, but I wasn't certain if she'd be going home after school or if she'd be staying for the haunted house. I supposed I could look for her that afternoon, and if I didn't run into her, I could try her at home over the weekend.

"You have to be the most adorable zombie I've ever seen," Cody said later that afternoon after he'd finished applying my makeup. He'd volunteered to help me get ready for the event at the school.

"Then you're doing it wrong. Zombies are supposed to be horrifying. Let me have that mirror."

Cody handed me the hand mirror on my dresser. I actually looked pretty awesome. Cody had done a fantastic job, just like he'd assured me he would.

"Where'd you learn to apply makeup like that?" I asked as I studied my reflection.

"I'm a man of many talents."

I smiled. "Yeah, you are."

"You, Caitlin Hart, are a tease. You know that your come-hither look makes me want to kiss you, but you also know that if I do, I'll end up with half your makeup on my face. Besides, that would make you late, and we don't want to keep the kids waiting."

"Later?" I asked.

"Later for sure."

Running around a fake haunted house in my fake zombie costume chasing real kids was the most fun I'd had in a long time. Who knew that channeling your dark side could be such a rush? Maybe I'd keep my zombie makeup on for my date with Cody later.

"Mike," I greeted Amanda's dad. "I'm so glad I ran into you."

"Cait?"

"Yeah, it's me under all this makeup. I wanted to see how you're doing with Angel."

"Actually," Mike smiled, "Angel is the best thing that has happened to Amanda and me in a long time. I guess I've been so knotted up with my own grief that I couldn't see how lonely Amanda was. Now that we have Angel to brighten up our lives we're both much happier. Thank you for taking the time to help me see what I couldn't on my own."

"You're welcome. I'm glad it worked out. I'm sure things have been tough for both of you."

"Yeah, they really have. I know it will take time for us to feel like our lives are back to some sort of normal, but in the meantime I feel like we're struggling to get through each day. Or at least we were. I won't say Angel has completely filled the hole that was created when my wife died, but Amanda seems to have a spring in her step that hasn't been there for quite some time."

"If there's ever anything I can do just let me know."

"Thank you. I appreciate that."

"I should get back. Have a wonderful time. We'll catch up later."

I looked around the room for Amanda. She was chatting with a group of girls about her age. I was so happy so see she was smiling and apparently having a wonderful time.

"Finn's looking for you," Velmalee informed me as I headed toward the entrance to scare a new batch of kids. "He's waiting down the hall in the front office."

"Okay, thanks." I turned around and headed down the hallway.

Finn laughed when I walked in. "You look adorable."

"I think the word you're looking for is terrifying."

Finn shrugged. "If you say so. I'm sorry to interrupt your brain eating, but I found something at Leif's. Something I think we should all take a look at."

"Do you want me to look at it now?"

"No, I think this is something we might want to look at as a group. I'm pretty sure it provides us with the motive we've been looking for."

"Okay. I'll get the gang together tonight. It will have to be after seven. I promised to eat brains till the end."

"That's perfect. I have some things to take care of anyway. I'll bring Chinese for everyone."

"Sounds good. Oh, and Finn…would you say Leif died prior to Bradley and Grover?"

"Yeah, it looks that way. Why?"

I shrugged. "I'm not sure, but somehow it seems important. I'll see you tonight."

Chapter 14

When I arrived at my cabin I found Siobhan sitting with Maggie on my deck, which overlooked the water.

I ran over and hugged my sister. "I thought you left!"

"I did. I went back to Seattle and met with the toad I realized I could never work with again for any amount of money. I knew he was a jerk, but somehow I guess I must have let myself forget that part of it. When he called me all I could think of was the fabulous corner office he was promising and the fact that I wouldn't have to move after all. Once I actually talked to him I turned him down flat."

"So you're back for good?" I asked hopefully.

"Maybe. Maggie not only agreed to let me stay with her for as long as I want but she offered me a job. It's only temporary, but it's enough for now."

"A job? You're going to work at the Bait and Stitch?"

The Bait and Stitch sold sewing and fishing supplies, neither of which seemed to be something Siobhan would be interested in.

"I'm going to be the mayor. It's a temporary positon until an election can be held, but I think it will be just the thing I need to help me move on."

"The mayor?" I asked. I looked at Maggie. "Can you do that? I mean, I know you're on the council, but can you just give the job of mayor to Siobhan?"

"Actually, I can. Or *we* can. The council as a whole, I mean. The island bylaws state that the council can replace members who die or must leave midterm by any means we deem necessary to conduct council business."

I did remember that from when Keith Weaver died while in office.

"The bylaws also state that the mayor will be chosen from among the current council members. I talked to both Francine and Byron, and they agreed Siobhan would make a wonderful interim council member until we get around to holding elections. And because none of us wanted to be mayor, we decided to offer the position to Siobhan. She'll need to run for and be elected to the position to keep it in the long run, but I know she'll be fabulous."

I had to agree. Siobhan would be the best mayor the island had ever had.

"And the fifth council member?" I asked. They still needed to fill the slot of the second man who had died.

"We plan to offer it to Drake Moore. He was the runner-up when Francine and I were elected. If he's no longer interested I guess we'll have to have a further discussion about it."

I hugged my sister. "Congratulations. I know you're going to be a great mayor."

"It'll be a challenge, but I like a challenge. I need a challenge. Besides, I feel like I need to completely reinvent myself and the island will be a good place to do that."

"Well, don't reinvent yourself too much; I like who you are, but I'm happy you're staying. I think everyone will be happy."

"Maybe most people will be glad I've decided to stay, but I'm not too sure about Finn. I called his cell, but he didn't pick up."

"He's coming over this evening. He said he had new information on the murder case. He's bringing Chinese. I need to run in and take a quick shower before everyone gets here. I washed the bulk of my makeup off in the sink in the girls' bathroom at the school, but I'm pretty sure I still have goop in my hair."

The new evidence Finn brought to share was disturbing. While he had been searching Leif's house for evidence as to who might have killed him, he'd found a video in the VCR. It showed Leif and Bradley on Leif's boat during a huge storm. On the boat with them was Jeremy Vance. Leif and Bradley were tormenting the poor guy. The beginning of the tape showed the older men teasing the younger one because he was puking up a gut as a result of the rough seas. Leif taunted the young man, insisting that a real fisherman would have better sea legs. Leif insisted that the fact that Jeremy was ill served as confirmation that he was lying about being a fisherman. The guy insisted he was, but Leif was having none of it. At one point Leif and Jeremy ended up in a fistfight. Initially it looked as if Jeremy was winning, but Leif hit him over the head with a metal pipe. Then he picked the guy up and tossed him overboard.

"Oh, God," I groaned. "I can't believe they killed him in cold blood."

"Leif could be a bit of a jerk," Danny confirmed. "Bradley too. I talked to Buzz Walton, and he told me that when the guy showed up and wanted to join the lodge, Leif flat out told him to go away. He said Jeremy said he'd looked up our bylaws and all that was required for membership was that the applicant be a resident of the island, male, and a fisherman or the descendant of one. He insisted he was male, a resident of the island, and a fisherman. When Leif asked Jeremy who he fished for, he gave him the name of a company from out of the area. He said he'd just moved to Madrona Island and really wanted to fit in."

I could totally imagine the men from the lodge shunning the younger man. They valued their old boys' club.

"Anyway, Buzz said the guy might have been a pest, but he did have a point, so they couldn't forbid him from attending lodge functions. According to Buzz, it was Bradley who had the idea of inviting him to the backroom poker game. I guess he figured they'd massacre him financially and he'd toddle away with his tail between his legs."

"But it didn't work out that way."

"Nope. He creamed everyone."

"Okay, so Bradley and Leif are on tape beating the kid before tossing him overboard," Siobhan began. "Who was doing the taping? Grover?"

"There's no way Grover was on that boat the night of the storm," I said with certainty. "He wouldn't even take the ferry. The guy was terrified of water."

"If Grover wasn't the person who did the taping then who else was on the boat and where did Grover fit into this?" Siobhan asked.

Cody laced his fingers through mine as we discussed the grisly murder of an innocent man. Part of me really wanted to solve this puzzle, but most of me just wanted everyone to go home so Cody and I could be alone together.

"Let's look at this systematically," Finn suggested. "Siobhan, why don't you flip the whiteboard over and draw a timeline of the relevant events as we know them."

Siobhan smiled at Finn and he smiled back. It looked like things were going to be okay between one of my favorite couples.

"We know Jeremy Vance was murdered by Mayor Bradley and Leif Piney during the big storm we had on September fifth."

"How do you know it was September fifth?" I asked.

"The video had a date stamp," Finn explained. "We also know Vance's body was found by the Coast Guard on September fourteenth."

I frowned. "The newspaper article Cody and I found indicated that Jeremy died of dehydration. It looked like he must have drowned when he was tossed overboard."

"The records I dug up indicate he did die of dehydration," Finn confirmed. "He must have been alive and conscious when he was tossed overboard. Somehow he made it to the island and died at some point after that."

"How awful." Tara shuddered. "He survived the ocean but died due to a lack of fresh water? It doesn't seem fair."

I had to agree.

"I didn't see either of the men drop a black poker chip into Jeremy's pocket in the film, so the chip must have been placed there by Jeremy at some prior time," Finn continued. "I spoke to several men who take part in the backroom game and they confirmed that black chips are used."

"Leif had a whole pile of them on the table in his house," I informed the group. "I wonder why. Doesn't everyone usually cash their chips in when the game's over?"

"Usually," Danny confirmed.

"Moving on with the timeline," Finn continued, "the medical examiner has estimated Leif's date of death as October sixteenth or seventeenth. His office is still running tests. Mayor Bradley died on October nineteenth and Grover died on the twenty-second."

"Did Leif have a black poker chip in his pocket?" Tara asked.

"No."

Everyone sat quietly for a moment while Siobhan caught up.

"We're assuming the deaths of the three men are related to what happened to Jeremy Vance," she began, "but if that's true, how does Grover fit into this? Was he a member of the poker group?"

"Grover joined the game occasionally but hadn't played lately," Finn said. "The men I spoke to all indicated that he was having financial issues, which we've already established to be true."

"Maybe the person who filmed the event is the killer," Cody suggested. "If we're assuming it wasn't Grover—and I think that's a safe bet—it seems like the fourth person on the boat that night would likewise be a victim, and the fact that we don't have another body could indicate that the person doing the recording hasn't been a victim because he's the killer."

"Okay, so how do we find out who the fourth person is?" I asked.

"I hate to even suggest this, but maybe we should look at the video again," Cody said. "The first time through we were all so horrified we weren't really looking for details."

"Good idea." Finn rewound the video and we watched it again and again.

"Pause it," Cody said the fourth time the horrible images played on my television screen.

Finn did.

"Look there." Cody got up and pointed to a reflection on the glass. It was faint but clearly visible.

I squinted. "It looks like Buzz Walton."

Chapter 15

Halloween

It had been two days since we'd thought we'd solved the mystery of who had killed Leif, Bradley, and Grover, but Ichabod was still with me, which seemed to hint at the fact that we might not have things as wrapped up as we thought. On every other occasion when Tansy had sent a kitty helper, the cat had been gone within hours of the mystery being solved.

Buzz confessed to killing Leif, although for whatever reason he insisted he didn't kill either Bradley or Grover. He told Finn that the events of the night on which Jeremy Vance had died had haunted him ever since. If Buzz was to be believed, the whole thing had been Leif's idea. A lot of the men at the lodge weren't thrilled that Jeremy had wormed his way into their sacred lair, but Leif was the most furious of all. When he heard a storm was on the way he'd convinced Bradley and Buzz that they would be justified in having a little fun with the guy. Buzz swore the plan had been simply to take him on a bumpy ride to prove he didn't have what it took to be a real fisherman. Buzz insisted they were only trying to scare him, but Leif had hit Jeremy with the pipe and tossed him overboard before he and Bradley even realized what was happening.

After a month of dealing with nightmares, he took the tape to Leif and insisted he was going to give a copy to the sheriff if Leif didn't turn himself in. Leif not only refused but attacked him. They struggled, and Buzz confessed that he pushed Leif, who hit his head. When Buzz realized Leif was dead he panicked and took off running.

Buzz's confession made perfect sense, but if he didn't kill Bradley or Grover we had a second killer. At first that seemed unlikely, but the more I thought about it, the more I thought that might have been just what had happened.

We never could figure out how Grover fit into things, and maybe that was because he didn't. If Bradley and Grover hadn't been killed by Buzz it made sense for us to return to our original theory that the business deal the men were involved in was in some way responsible for their deaths. But who, other than Maggie and I, had motive?

"What are we missing?" I asked my furry roommate.

Ichabod yawned.

"Did Cody and I keep you awake last night?"

Ichabod rolled onto his back. I thought about my night with Cody as I scratched the cat's belly. Things were going so well. I couldn't remember ever being this happy, despite the horrible things that had been going on.

"I suppose I should get up and get dressed," I said to my feline companion.

It was Halloween and the island was holding a celebration on Main Street, and Tara and I had decided to close the store so we could attend. Cody was coming by later to pick me up and I knew Tara planned to bring all three Paulson girls with her.

"I do wish I could figure out the last piece of the puzzle, though. I hate it when things are left hanging."

I crawled out of bed and headed downstairs to make some coffee. I studied Siobhan's murder board as I waited for it to brew. She really had had a good idea about using the board. She'd saved old motives and suspects off to the side as new evidence was brought forth in case we needed to go back to reconsider them. If Buzz hadn't been lying about killing Bradley and Grover that was exactly what we needed to do.

I remembered discussing the fact that it would take a compelling reason to get Bradley to go into the hollow. Assuming the mayor was lured to the ledge and then pushed, the killer would also need to have had access to the black poker chips because one had been found in both his pocket and near Grover's body.

I wandered into the kitchen as the coffee finished its cycle. I poured myself a cup and then went over to the window. I tried to figure out who would have all the pieces of the puzzle as I watched a flock of seagulls on the beach.

I felt like the killer was just beyond my reach. All I needed to do was put all the pieces together so a picture could emerge. I headed over to the murder board and began to list the things I knew for sure.

Assuming the removal of the cats was really the motive for the deaths of Bradley and Grover:

1. The killer would have to know about the project in the hollow.
2. The killer needed to have a strong conviction that the project shouldn't happen.
3. The killer would have to have something to use as a lure to get Bradley into the hollow and Grover into a boat.
4. The killer had to have access to black poker chips.
5. The killer had to have a reason to use the black chips; perhaps as some kind of a decoy?

I continued to study the board and suddenly knew exactly what had happened.

I hurried upstairs to get dressed. I was going to call Cody and Finn, but then I decided to check out my hunch first. If it turned out to be correct I'd call Finn.

When I arrived at my destination I hesitated. Maybe I should have called Finn and asked him to come with me. On the other hand, if Finn was with me the killer would probably clam up, and knowing what I did about my suspect, I doubted the killer could actually harm me. I knocked on the door and waited.

"Why am I not surprised to see you here?"

"Can I come in?" I asked.

"Sure. I guess."

I walked into the entryway and immediately began to regret my rashness. It sounded as if my suspect had been expecting me.

"What can I do for you?"

"I know what you did," I blurted out.

Smooth move, Cait.

"You can't prove anything."

That was actually a good point. I had no proof.

"Do you know what Mayor Bradley and Mr. Cloverdale planned to do?" the suspect asked.

I nodded and said, "I guess you must have seen the contract when you were cleaning Grover's home."

Lacy walked across the room and leaned against a secretary table that was positioned against the wall. "He really wasn't very careful about what he left lying around."

"Look, I know you love the trees and the cats. I do too. And I know why you felt you needed to do what you did. I can even relate to your feelings of anger. But killing two men seems like an extreme solution."

"Mayor Bradley and Mr. Cloverdale were going to kill the cats and then cut down all the trees. Those trees have been on the island longer than any of the settlers. It wasn't right. Someone had to stop them."

Suddenly I knew what *TLB* stood for. I'd heard Bradley refer to Lacy as a tree-loving bitch on more than one occasion when she'd tied up a council meeting with her protests any time a tree on the island was cut down for any reason.

"How did you get Bradley to meet you in the hollow?"

"I had leverage."

"The tape," I realized.

"I clean Leif's house once a week, or at least I did. I'll need to get a new customer now that he's dead. Anyway, I went to clean and found him dead on the floor, with the tape sticking out of the VCR. I knew who the guy in the video was. I remembered reading about his death in the newspaper. I saw the stack of poker chips, and suddenly I had the plan I'd been struggling to find."

I watched as Lacy slowly opened and closed the drawer next to the table where she stood. I was pretty sure she must have a weapon inside.

"So you called Bradley and told him you had the tape. I imagine you even described its contents, so he would know you were telling the truth. You told him to meet you in the hollow, I imagine to discuss the price of your silence. He couldn't refuse, so he made the trip and you pushed him off the ledge. Then you put a poker chip in his pocket to link his death to Leif's. Smart."

"I thought so, but I didn't realize it would take so long for someone to find Leif's body. I almost called it in myself, but I didn't want to call attention to myself."

"And Grover? What did you have on him to get him into a boat?"

"He was a little harder. I actually had more dirt on him because I cleaned his house, but he had a greater fear, so I knew I'd have to find something really scandalous. In the end I threatened to reveal something about his wife."

"His wife?"

"I found photos of her with another woman. They were old photos, most likely from before he even married her, but I was certain she wouldn't want them passed all over town."

I frowned. Mrs. Cloverdale and another woman? I would never have guessed that in a million years. She seemed so proper. I found it tragic that Grover had died trying to protect his wife's reputation.

"So what now?" Lacy asked. "Are you going to turn me in?"

"I think I have to."

"Even though the men were going to destroy the hollow for mere profit?"

"Even though."

Lacy opened the drawer she'd been playing with and took out a gun. "I'm sorry to hear that. I actually thought you might be more reasonable and see things my way."

"If you had dirt on both of the men why didn't you just use that to blackmail them into dropping the project in the hollow?"

Lacy frowned. "Yeah, I guess that might have worked as well."

I couldn't help but roll my eyes. The woman was a loon.

"But I didn't do it that way, so now I guess I need to clean up my mess."

Lacy pointed the gun at my head.

"The neighbors will hear the gunshot," I warned her.

Lacy hesitated. "I suppose that's true. Perhaps we should take this to the basement."

Lacy motioned for me to walk down the hallway, which I did. I just needed to figure out a way to create a distraction. Lacy told me to open the door to the basement and head down the stairs.

"The neighbors will still hear a gunshot from here," I reasoned.

"No, they won't."

Lacy flipped on the light.

"What is this place?" The room was padded with a thick black material and there were chains hanging from the walls.

"It's my playroom. It's soundproof; no need to share my sessions with the neighbors."

"Sessions?"

"With men. I like it rough."

Ew.

Lacy pointed the gun at my head once again. "I really am sorry about this," she said as she pulled the trigger.

I screamed but nothing happened.

"Damn. I guess I'm out of bullets. Hang tight; I'll be right back."

Lacy headed up the stairs. I hoped she wouldn't lock the door behind her, but of course she did. I looked around the basement for something to use as a weapon. There were plenty of props but nothing that was going to win out against a gun.

I had to face it: I had no option but to wait for Lacy to come back and shoot me. I couldn't try to overpower her; she outweighed me by fifty pounds. I couldn't try to talk her out of it; she'd already killed two men, so I doubted there was much I could say to change her mind.

I paced around the basement and waited. I didn't want to die. I finally had the relationship with Cody I'd always dreamed of. I needed more time. *We* needed more time.

I began searching the walls for something—anything—that would give me a chance. Even a slim one. I couldn't just stand there while she ended my life.

What in the heck was taking her so long? She'd made it sound like she was simply heading upstairs for bullets. Maybe she was completely out. Maybe she had to go out for more. Maybe someone would rescue me after all.

The minutes turned to…well, probably more minutes. I was sure I hadn't been there an hour, although in many ways it felt that long. I paced and I prayed. Really, what more could I do?

"Sorry that took so long," Lacy said as she came back into the basement. "There was someone at the door. Now, where were we?"

Lacy pointed the gun at my head once again. I was willing to bet she had bullets this time.

"Wait!"

Lacy lowered the gun. "Wait for what?"

"I'm not sure the trees are as safe as you think they are," I improvised.

"Why not? Bradley and Grover are dead."

"Yes, but there was a third partner," I lied, hoping Lacy was as dumb as she appeared to be.

"I didn't see a third partner listed on the paperwork."

"He was a silent partner."

Lacy lowered her gun slightly.

"Let me go and I'll tell you who it is," I tried to negotiate.

"How about I kill you and then look into it myself?"

Lacy raised her gun again.

"It's Buzz Walton."

Lacy scrunched up her nose. "Really? Buzz Walton? Why would Buzz be in on the deal? He doesn't own any of the land in the hollow."

"Bradley cut him in."

"Why on earth would Bradley do that?"

"Did you ever stop to ask yourself who was behind the camera the night Jeremy Vance died?"

Lacy hesitated. She lowered her gun just a bit. "Buzz?"

"Yep. Buzz was going to go public with what he knew, so Bradley agreed to give him a cut. A big one. I bet he continues without the others. You know how badly Buzz needs money."

Lacy bit her lip. "He does need money. I guess I never thought about the person behind the camera. Thanks for the information."

Lacy raised her gun again.

"You're still going to shoot me?"

"You know too much. I really am sorry. I quite enjoyed killing Bradley and Cloverdale, but this isn't going to be nearly as much fun."

I closed my eyes as Lacy began to pull the trigger. I heard a loud bang, but I still felt alive. I opened my eyes to see Cody rushing toward me. Finn was cuffing Lacy.

"How did you find me?" I asked once Cody let go of me enough so I could breathe.

"I showed up at your place early. I saw the murder board and the notes you'd made. When I realized you were gone I figured you'd done exactly what you did, so I called Finn. We weren't sure where you'd gone, so we called Tara. She saw your car out her window. She came over here to try to stall Lacy until we could get here. Oh, God, Cait, I thought I'd lost you."

Cody hugged me again before he led me up the stairs and into Tara's waiting arms.

Chapter 16

"You know, Cody spent fifty bucks trying to win those two pink hippos," Tara said as we watched him attempt to master the ring toss.

"Oh, at least."

"It was really sweet of him to offer to win stuffed toys for Serenity and Trinity after Jake won a bear for Destiny."

"It *was* nice. It's too bad he's so incredibly horrible at carnival games," I added. "I could have won the toys for a couple of bucks each."

"Please tell me that you aren't going to point that out when he comes over."

I just smiled.

"Caitlin Hart, you are truly soulless."

"I *am* dressed as the devil."

Cody and I had come to the street festival with Tara and the Paulson girls. Jake had met up with Destiny after we arrived. Siobhan was off somewhere with Finn and Danny was conspicuously absent. I could tell by the look on Tara's face that she wasn't pleased by the situation, so I didn't ask.

"It seems like you and Cody are … well, it just seems as if you are."

"Sleeping together."

Tara looked at me and grinned. "You are, aren't you?"

"I'll never tell."

Tara hugged me. "I'm so happy for you guys. You know I've been rooting for you to get together. If there's a couple on earth that's truly meant for each other it's the two of you."

I looked at Cody as he passed the guy yet another twenty. What was he doing? He'd already won the two hippos he was after. He was going to have to take out a mortgage on the paper if he kept this up much longer.

"It seems like Siobhan and Finn might have worked things out," Tara commented.

"Yeah, I think they have. I guess it's too early to say for certain whether they'll be able to get back to where they were before she stomped all over his heart, but it does seem they've at least settled into a friendship."

"Relationships are complicated." Tara sighed.

"Do you want to talk about it?"

"Let's suffice it to say that Danny and I are taking a break from whatever it is we've been doing, which never actually has been defined."

"I'm sorry. Is there anything I can do?"

"No, not really."

Apparently, Cody must have managed to get the right ring on the right peg because Serenity and Trinity were jumping up and down and clapping and screaming when I walked up.

"Cody only needs one more ring to win the monkey," Trinity shouted across the pavement.

"I think Cody is going to make some little girl a wonderful father," Tara said.

"Yeah." I smiled. "I think you're right."

"It's weird, but ever since Destiny moved in with me, I've started to think about having kids," Tara shared. "Not immediately, but sooner rather than later. I guess that's part of the reason I decided to take a step back from pursuing things with Danny. I'm not sure he's the settling-down type."

"I'm sorry, but I can't disagree with you. At least not at this point in his life. I keep half-expecting Danny to take off to Alaska with Aiden one of these summers."

"For you, my lady." Cody walked up and very proudly handed me a stuffed monkey. I didn't have the heart to rib him about the amount of money he'd spent to win it, like I'd planned to.

"Thank you. I love it." And I really did.

"Where to now?" Cody asked.

"Ice cream," Serenity suggested.

Cody looked at me.

"I could do ice cream."

"Ice cream it is."

Cody took Trinity by the hand. There was no doubt about it; I'd found myself a pretty perfect guy.

When Cody and I returned to my cabin we realized it was time for Ichabod to go home. There was a small part of me that hoped he'd stay, but deep in my heart I knew he wouldn't. They never did. Ichabod greeted us as we went inside, but then immediately began scratching at the door. When I opened it he walked over to my car and waited patiently for me to let him inside.

"I think it's time," I said to Cody. "Would you like to come with me?"

"Sure. Where are we going?"

"I don't know. I'm sure Ichabod will show us the way."

"Show us the way? How?"

I smiled. "You'll see."

Cody and I drove through town. A lot of the locals had strung orange and white lights and decorated their yards with scarecrows and sheets formed like ghosts. Almost every porch had a jack-o'-lantern, and a few houses had gone all out with dry ice, cemeteries, and killer zombies at the door.

We followed Ichabod's directions through town and north. Eventually, he had us pull off onto a narrow drive that we followed to the end. The house was small and old but well-kept. I let Ichabod out of the car and walked up to the door with him.

I knocked and an old man answered.

"Well, I'll be." He looked down at Ichabod.

The cat walked into the house and trotted down the hall.

"I take it Ichabod is your cat?" I asked, just to be sure.

"I guess he is now."

I frowned. "What do you mean?"

"My grandson Billy is sick. Leukemia. He's responding to the treatment, but his spirits are diminished after so much suffering. He was very disappointed he couldn't go trick-or-treating with the other kids, but his energy is low and I didn't want him to overdo it. I heard him saying his prayers after I put him to bed. He asked God to bring Halloween to him. He specifically asked for a Halloween cat. And the next thing I know, there's a Halloween kitty on my doorstep."

I was sure I was going to cry.

"Ichabod is a very special cat," I said to the old man. "I can assure you that if Ichabod is here to help Billy, he'll be feeling better in no time."

USA Today best-selling author Kathi Daley lives in beautiful Lake Tahoe with her husband Ken. When she isn't writing, she likes spending time hiking the miles of desolate trails surrounding her home. Find out more about her books at www.kathidaley.com

94785428R00115